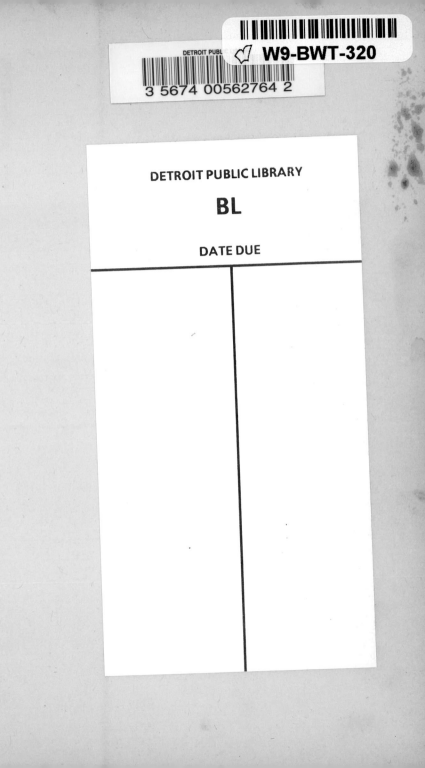

THE SARDINIAN SMILE

BOOKS BY PETRU DUMITRIU

Family Jewels

The Prodigals

Incognito

The Extreme Occident

The Sardinian Smile

The Sardinian Smile

BY PETRU DUMITRIU

Translated from the French by Peter Green

HOLT, RINEHART AND WINSTON

NEW YORK   CHICAGO   SAN FRANCISCO

d. 3

Designer: Ernst Reichl
8725152
Printed in the United States of America

He had the Sardinian smile

—Balzac, *Albert Savarus*

Three members of a family move towards tragedy as the love of a mother for her son turns to obsessive devotion, and the father is excluded and ignored.

THE CHILD'S laugh rang out from one end of the beach to the other. Though my eyes were closed, I could picture the whole scene: the deep sky far above my outstretched body, its blueness dimmed by a light gray haze from the evaporation of this all-too-salty sea; steep hills clustering around a sandy cove and watching over it, muzzles on paws, with a jealous and disturbing vigilance. Above those snoutlike rocks, the rounded hilltops, and covering them a layer of coarse undergrowth, brown by the summer sun. The hills pressed in on the cove with an evil persistence, as though stalking it: one felt besieged. Yet some magic interdict had halted their advance at the edge of the beach, which enjoyed a miraculous immunity. The sea would never overwhelm the beach; the hills would never break loose from their crouching immobility and pounce, at long last, raking it with their claws of shale. It would remain like this forever, between the sea and the sky and the ravines, in serene and eternal isolation, the muted murmur of the surf a ground bass overlaid by chirping cicadas and the musical drone of bees.

I ran the palms of both hands caressingly over the sand, and its heat spread gently through the flesh of my hands and the sensitive skin on the underside of my forearms. When the heat had been absorbed from the sand into my body, I would shift my arms and hands to some other spot where it was still undiminished. So I traced a series of large circles around my body in the sand. The effect resembled Leonardo's sketch of man inscribed naked within a sphere; but whereas his eyes are open and his expression somewhat stern, my eyelids were tight shut and I lay smiling up at the sun, wide open to its full force. Its heat lay on my chest and face and shoulders and belly and thighs like some warm, heavy, impalpable body.

Burning purity, a still radiance, fierce, simple, dazzling. It was then, at that precise moment, that the child's laughter rang out and went echoing on through the silence. It was something quite apart from the terrible sun and fiery air, marvelously fresh, more liquid than the sea and so distinct from it, wholly alien to those heavy, silent hills, so clear and light and radiant that I smiled behind my closed eyes, as though I had been granted a revelation of pure spirit, a brief ecstatic moment of mental euphoria. There was a dancing, positively aerial delight about such gaiety.

The little boy's laughter spread along the beach, growing louder as he approached me. I opened my eyes and raised my head, smiling, curious to find out what was amusing the child, eager to share in his delight. I could never have laughed like that. I had let myself become filled with the tender yet pitiless spirit of the south, consciously identifying and integrating my outlook with it. But the boy and his laughter partook of a colder, purer, more exalted spirit. One glance at his slender body— the sun never succeeded in getting it properly brown—was enough for me to see this. He was more spirit than flesh. His skin had a pale amber glow about it; his short smooth hair was so fair it seemed almost like silver. Everything about him looked different, alien—those slender limbs, the rib cage jutting from behind its delicate envelope of skin, the neat flat stomach, tiny muscles just visible here and there on its surface, the miniature bulge beneath it. His whole substance set him apart from this mineral, solar world in which the very vegetation had been calcined to a consistency much like that of stone or ash, its aromatic sap fast seeping away through every pore.

He, on the other hand, was running and laughing. Amid all this watchful stillness, where even the weary backflow of the waves on the shore had become a mere rhythmic hypostasis of inaction, this sprinting, urgent figure stood out incongruously. Above all, his laughter shattered the silence I had just immersed myself in—even to the point of shutting my eyes to gain any last extra degree of stillness that might be created by the shadows behind my eyelids and the voluptuous torpor of my body. And in this quietude, which the murmur of the surf and countless droning insects entirely failed to disturb, there now pealed out the fragile yet triumphant proclamation that was his laughter.

He was running in my direction, still laughing; just as I looked he glanced back at his father, who was in hot pursuit of him. His father did not look at all amused, but rather angry and irritated. He was a very big man, with wide, heavily muscled shoulders and a thick mat of hair on his chest. His long, powerful thighs were hairy too, and his body had much the same color, though with a reddish tinge to it and a sparse sanding of freckles. His hair was blond, like his son's, but ashen and lusterless. Everything about him was duller, from his complexion to the pupils of his eyes, blurred now by advancing middle age. He had the same jutting forehead, the same straight eyebrows, the same deepset eyes placed high up under the orbital ridge. But all his features were stamped in a heavier mold, especially the lower part of his face, which looked a little too lined and fleshy, the skin dark with a heavy growth of beard.

He was wearing a dirty, faded pair of bathing trunks that should have been thrown away long before and fitted him very badly. His violent movements as he ran had made some seam or elastic band give way; for the last few seconds his heavy, brownish-purple scrotum had been plainly visible, bouncing against the side of his thigh. This uncouth and farcical sight sent the boy into helpless gales of laughter. He stopped, panting, quite incapable of running any farther. His father caught up with him in a flash, seized him in one hand—the neat, slim little golden body flattened against that monument of hairy muscle—and gave him a tremendous spanking, the vast paw that executed justice dwarfing the child's entire backside. It was all over very quickly: a brisk volley of smacks, applied with a staccato rhythm that sounded as mechanical as that of the waves, though a good deal faster, and formed an accompaniment—without ever interrupting it—to the laughter, crescendo and diminuendo by turns, of the boy himself.

I let my head drop back on the sand and shut my eyes again. I just had time for a quick glimpse of them after they separated: the boy naked, laughing still but close to tears and rubbing his reddened buttocks while the father stamped off in a fury. I let myself slide back into the dim-shadowed world of heat and stillness and filled my nostrils with the scent of mint and seaweed and honey dew floating in the air. I sought refuge in my drowsy, half-sleeping state, partly out of indifference, partly from tact. I had no wish to watch while my host adjusted his dress, no wish to become involved in some minor conflict between him and his son. Blindly exploring the sand around me, I once more became aware of the sun's body pressing down on mine.

I have never found out what provoked this unimportant incident. Both father and son had undoubtedly forgotten all about it by the following day. I find myself wondering, in some surprise, just why it fixed itself in my memory. Even now, in retrospect, it requires some effort to see it as a portent for the future—which, indeed, it never really was—or as a symbol; but a symbol of what? Perhaps it *was* some kind of sign, but I remain properly skeptical about this. I know what I would like to see in the episode: the triumph of childhood, of everything that is new and unpolluted, fragile yet containing all the strength of the future over the power, authority, and dignity (the last decidedly in abeyance just then) of fatherhood, of the world even. Across my memories of the beach, the sea, the hills, the sun, flashes this childish laughter, untinged by irony or malice, pure gaiety confronting I know not what unjust and vaguely ridiculous anger. I see it now as an innocent protest against the whole of creation and, beyond this, as a fleeting triumph over the stern, incomprehensible God we have made in our own

5

image and whose very existence remains uncertain.

No, such an attempt at interpretation is doomed in advance, and I am forced to abandon it. Myths have no real value; symbols are at best a rough approximation of the truth. Words can only give a remote and highly equivocal indication of that ineffable reality that nothing but an inarticulate cry—in the moment of utterance—can account for with any fidelity. So one is left with the midday scene and the boy's laughter when confronted with those grotesque attributes of potency, fatherhood, and the generative act. A laugh still unsullied by any awareness of good and evil, free from the burden of knowledge; a free, untroubled laugh that made no attempt to deny this looming pile of rocks and waves and sand and heat and sunshine, did not even seek to free itself from them but was content merely to exist, to *be*, as alien in its substance from them as it was from the terrible yet ridiculous person of paternal justice. To be—who knows?—something more than all these things.

But, I repeat once more, I must have the courage to dismiss such idle speculations and admit that there is no *reason* why I happen to remember this particular incident, just as there is no reason why I choose to mention it now; or if there is, it eludes me.

We went in for another swim and then, with the high summer sun beating down on us, made our way up to the house by the steps flanking the hillside: huge flags of rough-hewn stone, so big I cannot imagine how they were ever transported there, even had they been quarried from the rocks nearby. The Sardinians, like their ancient enemies the Romans and their cousins the Italians, have always been much addicted to Cyclopean stone building. In this they much resemble the Maltese, to whom they are still more closely bound by secret and age-old ties of kinship and who—humble country folk that they are—quite recently, less than three centuries ago, built a church at Mosta, an ordinary village in the middle of the island, with a dome larger than that of St. Paul's in London and not the least bit inferior to those of St. Peter's in Rome and St. Sophia's in Constantinople.

Yet my admiration at the size of this achievement was eclipsed by my feeling of distress at its futility. The construction of these unnecessary steps had involved too much sweat and labor, the quarrying and transport of too many all-too-heavy stone slabs. No one in the village could say at what period the steps had been built or by whom. But the work had certainly not been done by slaves or serfs; the Sardinians have always been a free peasantry. For what purpose were these hundreds of steps originally set in place? There was nothing at the top except the house belonging to the vineyard and my host's modest estate. The bay below was too small and, above all, too isolated by those hostile hills to be used by fishermen. Smugglers were hardly likely to build such an enormous ramp. It was a monumental achievement, though now somewhat worn and dilapidated, with broken pointing, sunken or displaced flags, and holes through which balm and lavender sprouted. What remained indestructible was the crude vigor and the absurdity of these interminable steps, so majestic and so pointless in their ascent. The stone was mica schist, dark-textured, glinting with flecks of gold. The sun had made it so hot I could never have walked on it barefoot. I felt its burning surface right through the soles of my sandals.

We climbed in silence, the boy practically running, his father panting a little. I myself was badly winded, despite the fact that I was only twenty at the time. In marked contrast to my host—a blond, statuesque giant of a man in his mid-forties—I was very much out of training.

He had nothing on except an old pair of cotton trousers and open sandals. It surprises me that I retain so vivid a memory of both him and the boy —that vast torso, gleaming with perspiration as he walked beside me, lungs drawing in deep drafts of air, while the child's small delicate figure almost danced from one step to the next—yet I have quite forgotten the boy's mother. Probably she did not accompany us to the beach that day—or else she had gone off somewhere, as she so often did, to lie naked in the sun behind the rocks or among the tall bushes that exuded an aromatic sap when the sun was at its height.

It was on one such occasion that her son had seen her, or was to see her, either before or after the morning I have just described; I cannot place the incident with any precision. Much later he revealed the fact to his father. But that was at the beginning of his farewell letter, when they were destined never to speak to one another again.

There he was then, a young boy wandering naked along the beach, looking for shells, walking over the firm sand with its tiny wavelike ripple marks, from which, every now and again, a tiny flash of light would catch his eye, the sun reflected in a grain of mica. Then he plunged into the bushes, often moving sideways, not bothering to push the springy branches away with his hands but dodging them as though he were some lithe and slender toreador avoiding the horns of an invisible bull. Here, among the scented axillae of stalks and leafage, hornets and wasps and wild bees droned from flower to flower, minuscule furred heads shining golden as they sipped. The boy made daring passes at the tangled green undergrowth. Sometimes it brushed him momentarily, caressing his slim flanks and chest, his flat, colorless nipples, with its tender spear-shaped leaves.

Suddenly he was brought up short by the bright, white presence of naked human flesh. All he actually *saw*, as he wrote afterward, were those pale thighs, spreadeagled toward the sun, as though in the presence of a lover or a doctor or someone who was both at once.

Observe, he wrote, *that I do not speak of "a grimace." What happened, though it made no sound, was a cry, a harsh, wounded scream. It exploded silently in the middle of my chest. (I had a very delicate chest at the time, you will remember.) I was not afraid. I did not feel horrified. There was just this silent shock, right inside my body. A sense of consternation. For a brief moment my breath failed, my heart stopped beating. It was as if my very existence had been momentarily suspended. No embarrassment or timidity, simply the sure knowledge that what confronted me was something forbidden and alien. This red and howling source of power that was, at one and the same time, a gaping weakness, a death wound, lying there on the sand—none of this was for me. Only*

9

the shock, the impulse to remove myself. But I did not run away. I did not recoil. I turned and walked off slowly.

I have summoned up the hateful resolution to tell you this only so that you will understand what I am going to do once I have finished this letter. I am not trying to win your forgiveness, much less hers. She should never have let herself be seen like that. Oh, I know she had sought out an isolated spot. But not isolated enough. I know she claimed to be indisposed and said the sun did her good. I know that, strictly speaking, she was not responsible for the wound that the sight of hers inflicted on me. But perhaps, despite everything, there can be a degree of culpability in certain kinds of innocence, some kinds of distress that must never be inflicted, whatever the circumstances. In that case I am as culpable as she, since we are both equally innocent. I do not judge her. I love her. My heart is overflowing with tenderness and pity for her. You know that she is for me, as for you, the best and most beautiful woman in the world, the one capable of moving us most deeply, above all the one who has our greatest love. It is because of the love and tenderness and compassion I feel for you both that I am writing now instead of acting without explanation. This way you will at least understand.

WHEN I first became a student, just before the war, I enrolled for two terms at the University of Uppsala in order to attend Carl-Gustav Enquist's course of lectures on megalithic civilization. He noticed me and invited me to his house, and a friendship sprang up between us. I became a regular visitor. Finally he asked me to spend the summer vacation with him and his wife and his young son on the west coast of Sardinia. Subsequently I continued my archaeological studies at Rome, so that every summer I contrived to spend a few days or weeks in their company. There was even a period when I fell a little in love with Mme. Enquist. To my great surprise, I saw Carl-Gustav gradually abandon his academic career altogether and bury himself more or less permanently in this tiny Sardinian village, which not even the tourists bothered to visit. When, long afterward, I dared to inquire what motives he had had for doing this, his reply was so frivolous, rambling, and contradictory that I remained no wiser than before.

He was very well off, mostly as a result of his marriage. His wife was one of the four daughters of a wealthy Göteborg shipowner. He had no need to pursue a university career, except out of a pure passion for scholarship. Gradually this passion dwindled in him, as did every other interest, with one single exception: the curious obsession he had for the very curious Mme. Enquist. I am scrupulous in the matter of friendship, and because I respect my friends I prefer not to analyze them. Therefore I observed the metamorphosis of Enquist and his wife without being fully aware that any such change had taken place. Between the time I first got to know them—Michael was only seven or eight then—and my recent final visit, more than ten years later, there was only one gap of any length, during the war. When I saw them again afterward, he was so different and she so unchanged (this very static quality of hers, in marked contrast to the insensible mutation all the rest of us had undergone with the years, was itself a kind of perverse and paradoxical transformation) that I was quite astounded. But that was nothing compared to my last visit.

Usually I took the boat from Civitavecchia to Cagliari and went on from there by train or bus, via Iglesias and Oristano. If I was not coming through Rome, I would embark at Genoa for Porto Torres and then catch the Sassari-Macomer bus. I am not sure whether the regular air link between Rome and Alghero was in operation then, but I rather think so.

As I traveled I would let the harsh, bare quality of the districts I passed through slowly permeate my being. Places with names like Villasurgiu and Logusimius and Foguduru and Murangianus and Casteddu and Nurra, rendered grimmer still by the Sardinian *u*, a primitive, strangulated *ou* sound, like the hoot of a nightjar. It creates as great a gap between the island dialects and ordinary pleasant-sounding Italian as there is between the masculine austerity of the people and landscape and the softer, more sensuous mainland. Even their sense of serious values is different. Only in the hard, dried-up inland regions of the Mezzogiorno, far away from the coast, or the parched center of Sicily or—above all—the weird congealed landscape of Malta will you find some slight echo of Sardinia's sounds and people and physical characteristics.

Noises here had a still core of silence, into which I would let myself slide and dissolve, hearing things vaguely, as though from a great distance, and occasionally, out of the corner of one eye, catching a glimpse of some worn, determined face. The jolting bus was packed with tough, stony-faced peasants and their taciturn wives, a great mass of bodies all clothed in the same coarse, heavy material, amid whom I too had my place. I sank myself in their conversation. The murmurous, intermittent sound passed into my skull, became a wordless interior drone. But if I glanced out of the window, I beheld a world that denied me all entry.

To the right rose a steep range of hills; on the left stretched the sea. It was late afternoon and cloudy. A scatter of black islands, sheer cliffs rising to rounded peaks, lay on the gun-metal surface of the water. In front of us, toward the west, the clouds were flat and barred, like vapor trails, and ringed with pale yellow light. Sea and islands were frozen in the same remote and savage desolation. On our right an endless succession of stony spurs, schist or granite or slate, frowning, almost colorless, still burning hot in the twilight, with perilous overhangs above the road. Sometimes the rocks would retreat a little way, dragging clumps of *maquis* in their wake, its frizzled spikiness hinting at thorn brakes. All along the route I glimpsed patches of thin soil breaking through the stones. Very often there were stretches of supporting wall to protect the road: stone walls, always stone, grained and glinting with mica, roughly built but made to last forever. On all sides one came upon these mighty piles of rock, monuments to man's too persistent and excessive toil—and all to what end? To prop up a rock face or, with equally sterile intent, to hold back the hills and keep clear this deserted and patently useless road, now gleaming with steely puddles after a rain, this solitary track on which one iron box passed by and faded in the distance.

On the other side, toward the sea, there were, I knew, other equally massive buttresses built up from the plain below. Caught between these great masses of masonry and the weight of the hills themselves, the road had hardened until its clay surface acquired the consistency and, as evening drew on, the neutral color of the rocks around it.

We traversed an endless series of sharp bends. As we negotiated each one, we could see the road zigzagging in hairpin turns around the next rocky promontory stretching down to the sea. There would be a glimpse of deserted beaches and beyond, stretching to the horizon, the cold, hostile gleam of the sea. Then the road began to climb. We entered a hollow, a kind of deep-shadowed shelter in the hills. I glimpsed trees and houses and a bell tower crammed in between the encircling peaks, with a series of sheer drops below them and scrub-laden hillsides on which the lighter irregular rectangles were allotments, set at so steep an angle that they could only be plowed laterally, each furrow running above or below its predecessor, never at the same level.

The bus pulled up and a couple of villagers got out. I collected my grip—its old, worn leather went very well with this bare landscape—and descended with them. One or two men stood lounging against a low stone wall like so many gray shadows, hands thrust deep in their pockets, staring at us. They exchanged a few words with the driver, never raising their voices. Then the bus set off again and vanished in the distance, leaving the usual clouds of stinking exhaust fumes behind it.

Lower down, under a high and massive retaining wall, pierced by a vaulted arch through which water poured in torrents during the rainy season, there was the village square, a small ugly church, and a close-packed group of houses. Beyond lay the beach, with fishing boats drawn up on the shingle and a bleak expanse of sea behind them. Where I now paused for a moment, grip in hand, cars flashed by all summer without stopping. There was nothing to see and no hotel to put up at. And even if these travelers *had* stopped here, they would never have been able to make any real contact with the people they imagined they were meeting and talking to. The locals would at once have withdrawn into themselves, remote, secretive, elusive, cut off by everything they were, all they knew and these foreigners would never know, separated from them, in the first instance, by language. You have to speak a different dialect wherever you happen to be in Sardinia—Gallura, Campidanèse, the Logudoro patois, not to mention all the special idioms of the remote mountain villages. Even here the fishermen had one special language of their own—they were of highly mixed origins, with ancient elements of Genoese and Spanish and Greek in their ancestry—while the villagers had another; and up on the Giara, that great plateau that began beyond the summit of the nearby hills, the shepherds, the only true Sardinians, could scarcely make themselves understood by the folk below in the valley. Or rather, they had no particular desire to have any communication with them at all but kept themselves to themselves, in deliberate self-isolation.

I turned to the right, my feet squelching over dead leaves and dried cow pats and scattered litter, and made my way to the other tiny village square. Between me and this square ran the same low wall I have mentioned earlier, against which the men who were out of work used to lounge in the evening, unlit cigarette ends drooping from the corners of their mouths. To cross it I had to climb three steps, great blocks of damp stone. The flagstones of the square were moist too. Under the plane trees—their long pods littered the ground in drifts—in the center of a high-rimmed octagonal basin, the Maddalena stood erect on her plinth, no taller than a ten-year-old girl but decked out in the gaudiest colors: ocher face, purple lips, black eyes, baroque draperies painted dark blue and red. From the plinth there projected a rusty iron spout, and out of the spout gushed a never-failing jet of water, so clear and fresh that the mere recollection of it makes me thirsty. The basin was always full to overflowing, and the surplus water trickled noiselessly over the rim, soaking the green and glistening flagstones.

A group of women with buckets and pitchers stood near the fountain, talking to one another in low voices. Ten paces off, at the other end of the little square, several men squatted under a house wall, staring at nothing. Two or three of them were singing half under their breath, so quietly that no noise could be distinguished from the thickening patch of shadow under the trees except the dark *ou* sound and a monotonous melody of uncertain tonal derivation—Berber, perhaps, or Basque.

16

This place was known simply as the Maddalena—
"I'm going to the Maddelena," they would say, or
"I met him at the Maddelena." It was squeezed
in between a pair of over-large and too-solidly constructed corner houses, their yellowish plaster
peeling off in large flakes.

I knew what these houses were like inside—
bare, filthy walls, clumsy wooden furniture made
out of big planks, looking as though it had been
squared off roughly with an adz, mildewed quilts,
images of the Virgin standing above a little oil
lamp that was kept alight night and day. Under a
row of low, massive vaults there was also a tavern
that smelled of barrels and cheap wine. The chilly,
vinous odor wafting from its doorway resembled
the wind that comes up when you open a cellar
trapdoor.

At the bottom of the square, between two houses
at right angles, a shadowy passageway opened
through the rocks. I plunged into it, my feet tread-
ing on great blocks that were already much thicker
than any ordinary flagstones. It was here that the
ravine began, without warning or transition, its
mouth flanked by those two high, yellow house
walls, slicing the hill in two as far as its summit.
On each side of it a line of steps had been cut in the
rock. Between them ran a third stepped wall, far
too large for human feet, constructed from well-
dressed blocks of gigantic masonry. This wall had
been built across the gorge in order to check the
descent of any great boulders washed down by the
heavy rains. Normally the hollow was dry as a
bone, but at such times it boiled up to its very rim
with a thick, muddy, foaming liquid, and there
might be up to half a yard of brown water lapping

around the Maddalena. But this would only last for one thunderous night of lightning and torrential rain, and the next day nothing would be left but a few pools of water, a layer of pebble-laden silt, and sometimes one or two rounded boulders, like the one I could now see against the foot of the first check wall. It must have bounded over all the others, starting at the top and finally coming to rest where it lay now without even damaging the stonework. Nobody seemed to repair or maintain these walls; indeed, nobody seemed to have built them. They were simply *there*, now and forever, erect, immovable, indestructible, their own weight ensuring their permanence.

The righthand flight of steps was in a bad state of disrepair. I avoided it and took the left. At some points the steps had been broken into several loose, jagged fragments. Here on the left the stonework was as good as new. Below me ran a series of high buttressed walls, each supporting a terrace. One of these terraces was an orchard with some twenty trees in it, another an olive grove that contained about a dozen olive trees, a third a vineyard planted with dwarf vines no larger than a man's hand. The wall was two or three times as high as the width of cultivated ground it supported.

I saw a square house, with square windows: the mayor's. Then two others, built very low, backed into the slope of the rock. Then one more large square-windowed building, the last to have electric light—though even down in the village itself a good many homes went without it. I crossed the ravine on a massive single-arch bridge. Beyond there was nothing to be seen but the upward slope of the gorge, choked with greenery and, far above, between the two walls of the col, a patch of pale sky and one distant star.

I climbed steadily on through the gathering dusk. To my right I suddenly came upon the Funtana de Janas—a tiny artificial grotto, dark and damp, where there was always an abundance of pure cold spring water. Old silver coins lay gleaming on the bottom, less than a foot below the surface of the pool; yet no one, not even the village urchins, would have dared touch them. They were offerings to *Les Jeannes,* the fairies no one had ever seen, but whom no one would risk offending. I walked straight on, but not before—almost without realizing it—I had become conscious of the strange brooding atmosphere that emanated from this pool in the niche. Its stillness had nothing in common with the ordinary silence now enfolding the thickets, both behind and ahead of it.

Carl-Gustav Enquist had had benches set up every fifty or hundred steps, for the benefit of his visitors. But this was in the early days, when he could still be energetic enough at intervals and was playing the part of the hospitable recluse. Now their wooden slats were mostly rotten, broken, or missing. I found one or two that would still bear my weight and sat down for a little to get my breath. Then I set off once more, changing my grip to the other hand when its weight began to drag on my shoulder. I was tired and fed up. Usually Carl-Gustav sent someone to meet me and help carry my luggage.

One more corner, and the steps left the ravine and began to climb the slope of the hill, among gnarled holm oaks and olive trees. I was now actually on Carl-Gustav's estate. For the last time I sat down and rested; from this bench I could see clear out over the sea to the horizon. If you turned the other way you found yourself facing a great shadowy O beneath an overhanging lip of rock. This was a cave, not a very deep one but dry and warm even in winter. It contained nothing but little piles of human excrement—discreditable witness to the habits of Carl-Gustav's day laborers and various passing shepherds.

I set off once more. I could already make out the shape of the house, just visible through the trees and undergrowth at the top of the rise. There it stood, perched on a base of great stone blocks that formed the walls of the storeroom, a squat, dumpy building, with small square windows and white-washed walls glimmering through the darkness. Not a light was showing. I made my way around the corner buttress of the storeroom, to a furious chorus of barking dogs. Then the smell of smoke, wafted down by the wind, reached my nostrils, and at last I saw a light—the merest glimpse, coming from the open door of the shack occupied by the peasants who worked the estate. Enquist had very soon tired of trying to make the place pay its way, and for some while he'd let them keep what meager profit they could extract from it in return for their services.

I called out to the dogs by name, to quiet them down. Just as I was doing this a woman appeared in the doorway and peered in my direction, shading her eyes with her hand—an age-old peasant gesture, but on this occasion pointless as well as naïve, since it was quite dark. She must have seen me as a dark silhouette outlined against the paler background of the sea. She withdrew into the hut

20

again. From her deformed back I recognized Ignazia. A man came out and stood just as she had done, staring toward the sunken track, half-hidden among the trees, at the end of which I had stopped. The dogs were all around me, and their barking had lost its hostility. They were beginning to sniff at my legs, tails wagging.

"Who's that?" the man called out.

The voice was not that of Ignazia's husband; it belonged to Pascal, his brother-in-law. I identified myself. The climb had exhausted me; my left shoulder was hurting so much I had begun to massage it. As an indication of my annoyance I addressed him by his surname.

"Tell me, Taureddu," I said, "why didn't you or Lupu come down to meet me at the Maddalena? Surely the professor told you I was coming?"

He came across to where I was, picked up my grip, and said in a surly voice, "The professor didn't tell us anything."

It was not much of an excuse. He moved off, and I followed him. "I wrote him a week ago saying I'd get here today."

At this Pascal Taureddu stopped in his tracks. He turned around. "You mean you don't know what's happened?"

"I haven't heard a thing. Tell me."

He turned his back again and walked on, shoulders bowed by the weight of my grip. He was not going in the direction of his employer's house. Surprised, I followed him. We went into a small room. It was warm inside; a wood fire was burning on the stone hearth. The whole place smelled of smoke and stale bread and poverty. The door into the next room stood ajar, and through it I glimpsed

21

a couple of beds made from heavy planks and covered with gray blankets. The smoky, white-washed walls glowed orange in the light of a single oil lamp and were covered by vast shadows. When I walked in, the women stood up and the shadows moved with them. Old Assunta was there, a gaunt, stern, ramrod-straight figure, never bareheaded, always dressed in brown or brown-gray or black. So were her two daughters—Ignazia, the hunchback, a tiny angular creature whose face was carved in planes of yellowing marble, with great, dark, liquid eyes; and Giusta, who was as tall and straight and silent as her mother and who owed her carriage to the pots or bundles she regularly carried on her head.

Pascal dumped my grip on the beaten-earth floor. "The *professore* hasn't heard what's happened, then?" he said.

I was not a professor, in any sense of the word; and Enquist himself, having never attained the status of *ordinarius,* laid no claim to the title either. But for politeness' sake and because we were educated people, scholars, they used to call both of us professor—and especially their master—almost every time they addressed us.

The women watched me with unwavering eyes, never saying a word. Clearly they did not want to talk. Neither did Pascal.

"What on earth's happened? Where are your employers? And where's Marteddu?"

Lupu Marteddu was Ignazia's husband. She smiled faintly in a way I did not like at all and said, with a vague wave of the hand, "He's out."

What could he be up to, prowling around in the dark? I pondered this for a moment. Then Pascal said, "Come with me, *professore*." He picked up my grip again and walked out.

I followed him and sensed that the women were all close on my heels. Outside the door stood a big block of wood with a chopper stuck in it, where they split kindling for the fire. The chopper was of an extremely ancient type, its blade curving back in a half-moon, the steel head extended beyond the haft to form a hammerhead. Somewhere out there in the night Lupu was wandering about or busying himself with heaven knows what private ploy. Perhaps he was quite near at hand and watching us. From the nearby stable came sounds of movement and heavy breathing, the kind of noise cattle make when they stir in their sleep or chew their cud. I caught a whiff of hay and manure and milk. It was quite clear to me that something serious and unusual had taken place. I gathered this from the offhand, almost insolent way Pascal opened the door and marched through into the house—a completely new phenomenon.

The house smelled stale, neglected. All the doors were open. It was dark inside. Only when we got to the back of the house did we find any light—a single lamp burning on Enquist's bedside table. He lay there asleep, mouth wide open, head slumped back on the pillow. I glanced around the room; it was wildly disordered. Clothes and underwear were scattered about the floor or draped over chairs. Empty bottles lay underfoot. A half-full bottle, together with a dirty glass, still stood on the table beside the lamp. From here my gaze returned to Enquist's face, deathly pale under several days' growth of beard. The walls were about as grubby as those in the shack and glowed with

23

the same soft orange radiance. Our shadows loomed gigantic across them in sharp black silhouette. Something was very odd about the way Enquist was snoring, and a sharp twinge of uneasiness passed through me. There was not the slightest sign of Mme. Enquist or Michael. I turned and cast a suspicious glance over the man and the three women. They were all staring fixedly at the sleeper's face, just as though I had not been there. I went over and put my hand on Carl-Gustav's forehead. It was quite cold and sticky with sweat.

"How long has he been like this?" I asked. "He's very sick—"

Old Assunta, her eyes still fixed on Enquist's unshaven face, murmured very quietly, almost without moving her lips, "*Sarragu de is moribundus ...*"

It was true; this highly unpleasant snore could all too well be described by the Sardinian word *sorrocrare*, which sounds very like the death rattle it signifies. I bent down and lifted the arm that dangled beside the bed. But this was a stupid gesture, as useless as Ignazia's attempt to shade her eyes in the dark: I have never known how to take someone's pulse. The arm flopped heavily back again, its fingers striking the floor. The air in the bedroom smelled sour: I became aware that the whole place reeked of vomit.

"Has he been like this for long?" I asked again.

"For three days," Pascal said.

Ignazia added, "He hasn't stopped drinking since it happened."

I turned quickly and looked at her. From the tone of her voice I got the impression she was smiling. It was true; her thin, tough features bore

24

the same barely discernible lopsided grin that had appeared when she mentioned her husband.

"Where is the *signora*? And *Signorino* Michael? Has anyone called a doctor?"

This time they did look at me. Perhaps they were astonished to hear me mention a doctor for a man who was in a drunken coma, who indeed seemed at death's door. But the faint surprise visible in their dark eyes soon faded and was replaced by the original expression of blank impassivity they had greeted me with. Clearly they had no desire to discuss either the *signora* or her son. Later, when I found out what had happened—or at least, their version of that incident—I understood why. In their position I would have preferred to say nothing myself.

I felt I must find some way to help them overcome their reluctance. "Follow me," I said curtly.

I went back through the empty house, picking my way in the darkness among the disordered furniture. Pascal, the last person through the front door, slammed it carelessly behind him.

Outside in the courtyard I glimpsed a black, motionless silhouette. "Is that you, Lupu?" I called.

The moment the words were out, I regretted having addressed him in so familiar a manner. I was exhausted, uneasy, thoroughly alarmed by Carl-Gustav's condition, and enraged at the strange way they were all behaving. I could have kicked myself for committing such a tactical blunder with Lupu, of all people. He had always irritated me and had the knack of making me react in a manner wholly different from what I intended.

"Good evening, *professore*," he said. He neither

25

moved nor raised his voice. He was not a big man, and one could tell how strong he was only by this trick he had of standing stock-still, as though rooted to the ground, like some carved-stone figure with all the weight and solidity of a boulder. Nor did I like the way he stood his ground and waited for me to come to him. But I was familiar with his brand of coolly gratuitous bad manners by now. Enquist found him an unending source of amusement and used to snicker at his rudeness with an air of protective complicity.

Lupu's oafish behavior annoyed me so much that it was Pascal I sent off down to the village, carrying a note I had hastily scribbled at the kitchen table. I requested the postmistress to call up the nearest town and have a doctor sent out at once, by taxi if there was no car available. Expense was no object. The doctor should be warned that he would in all likelihood have to deal with a case of alcoholic coma. Pascal was to wait until she got through, so he would know what time he had to be at the Maddalena. From there he would guide the doctor to the house with a lantern.

When Pascal had gone, I turned my attention to the three women. Only Giusta looked a little less stony-faced, with some faint glimmering of humanity in her expression. They were all waiting for me to say something—though not with any great interest, since they knew much more than I did. I deliberately tried to stare Lupu out. He did not so much as blink. He was a square-chinned man, with a flat forehead and a thin gash of a mouth. Heavy muscles bunched around his jaw-line. His eyes met mine, direct, unwavering, yet quite devoid of expression.

26

"Well?" I said.

He did not stir; for a moment I thought he had not even heard me. Then, very slowly, he turned his head toward his wife. It was she who spoke at last—not the old woman or Giusta, neither of whom seemed to be listening. I know, now, that they did not *want* to listen. They knew that Ignazia was lying, in the sense that her version of events omitted part of the truth. Even if Lupu had not been there, even had she been subjected to torture and imprisonment, she still would not have revealed more than she told me that evening. But the last straw, I must admit—I did not realize it at the time, though I am quite sure of it now—was Lupu himself. There he sat on his bench, leaning back against the wall, hands spread flat on his thighs, not moving a muscle, utterly indifferent to what she was telling me, despite the fact that it directly concerned him. But this too I only discovered afterward. I even seem to remember him lighting a cigarette.

The story Ignazia unfolded, incomplete and slanted though it was, still revealed enough of the truth to fill me with consternation. Horrified, I plied her with further questions, but she had told me all she intended to. From then on she simply repeated her previous statements. Her mother and sister, under pressure, did no more than refer me back to Ignazia's narrative.

The dogs outside began barking, and Lupu went to see what was up. There was a murmur of voices, and in walked the local police sergeant, removing his official peaked cap as he crossed the threshold. *Maresciallo* Atzeni bore a slight resemblance to Lupu, though his expression was less forbidding.

He nodded to me, then sat down on the bench beside Lupu, his back against the wall, hands resting on his knees. He was swarthy-complexioned, with ruddy cheeks, a big, open face, and a bullet head. Like the others, he was a local man. "We're working on the case," he told me. Hadn't I heard anything about the *avvenimenti*? It had all been in the papers. Assunta came over, a glass of wine clutched in one gnarled hand, and offered it to him. They were working on the case, he repeated, his voice cold and official. He took the wine without a word of thanks, drank it down, and wiped his mouth with the back of his hand. A terrible business, he went on. Some outsider must have been responsible, no doubt about it. No one from the village. The village was a peaceful place. Nothing ever happened there.

When he stopped talking there was a general silence. *"No one,"* Atzeni repeated after a moment, "not even the folk up there in the hills, the shepherds. I know them all."

None of the women had said a word since he came in. Suddenly Ignazia spoke up, her gaunt features brightening with cunning and effrontery. "A couple of strangers were seen prowling about on the Giara that day."

Atzeni shot her a glance but did not condescend to reply. He had no wish to tell a direct lie. He would keep his mouth shut and turn his head the other way, but he would not demean himself to acquiesce in Ignazia's deliberate falsehood. I did not realize this, but now, looking back on the scene, I find it all as clear as day. Atzeni was paying no attention to Lupu. It was on my account that he had come—not to reassure me, but rather to neu-

28

tralize me, to wall me in, just as they did with their fields and roads and fountains. With themselves. Someone had seen me getting off the bus. One of the women I had seen by the Maddalena, with their buckets and pitchers, or maybe Pascal himself—honest, simple, harmless fellow that he was—had hurried off to find Atzeni, at the police station or wherever else he may have been, and warn him of my arrival.

After scrutinizing me seriously and attentively for a moment, the sergeant rose and took his leave. I know now that he wanted to be sure of my intentions—or rather, to make certain there was nothing I could do. It did not strike me at the time, but I realized afterward that throughout he had not once mentioned the *professore*. In the first place, any show of pity for him would have compromised not only Atzeni's own dignity, but that of Enquist himself. Such compassion was unthinkable in the circumstances. It is also possible that the sergeant was consumed by the same feeling of contemptuous anger and silent indignation I thought I had detected in Pascal.

My own reaction was a mixture of shocked distress, the misguided conviction that I now knew the whole truth—though, indeed, what I had heard was disconcerting enough in itself—and a barely conscious uneasiness provoked by something more in the atmosphere. I tried to explain away this uneasiness by attributing it to my irritation when faced with the reactions of these taciturn peasants—reactions that differed so radically from my own. This, I told myself, was why I wanted to walk out there and then, turn my back on the lot of them.

I asked Giusta—the only person present who did not fill me with this sense of angry impatience —to light the lamps in the big house, make me up a bed, and tidy the *professore*'s room a bit. Then I briefly bade them goodnight and left. I crossed the courtyard—tidy, deserted, with the big chopping block in the middle and a sheer wall beyond it, invisible now in the darkness. The wooded slope fell away steeply below me. Above the black tree tops I glimpsed the sea, blurred by clouds toward the horizon. A cold wind was blowing. The house stood there, a pale, secretive cube, waiting for me.

I walked in and wandered from room to room. The beds were still unmade. Here a dress lay draped over the back of a chair, there I passed an overturned armchair. The floor around Carl-Gustav's work table was littered with papers. Some of the loose leaves lying on desk or floor bore traces of dried vomit. Giusta, who had just lit the lamp, was squatting down in her homespun skirt, preparing to gather up all this stuff pell mell.

I said, "Here, leave that, I'll do it myself."

I was feeling thoroughly depressed, needed some kind of definite action to occupy my mind. Besides, I had recognized Enquist's handwriting. Was it possible he had begun working again? But a glance through the papers showed that despite the number of sheets, far too many of them for an ordinary letter, this was in fact some sort of communication addressed to his wife. I gathered up the sheets mechanically, without attempting to get them in the right order. They had not been numbered. All I meant to do, at first, was leave them in a pile under a paperweight, the neolithic grain mortar Enquist used as his ashtray. Then I noticed that some of the sheets were written in a different hand.

I do not make a habit of reading letters addressed to anyone other than myself. But in the circumstances, with the *avvenimenti* that had taken place and Carl-Gustav's present condition, I felt I could legitimately go through them. It was hours before the doctor arrived, and afterward I could not get to sleep. I spent all night reading. There was a letter from Michael to his father; a genuine letter this, in content and form. There was also what Carl-Gustav had written to his wife, at a time when he knew very well that she would never read any letter from him again. This fact alone betrayed it as the work of a deeply disturbed mind—a verdict that its incoherence, wild handwriting, and general tone merely served to confirm.

Next morning, long after the doctor had come and gone, I went out for a moment to get some fresh air. A high wind was blowing; the sea was ribbed and gray. From such a height the crests of the waves could barely be distinguished. The steep-cliffed islands on my left, away toward the southwest, looked bare and desolate. Dead leaves rustled across the terrace. Full of anxiety, I stood contemplating this limitless expanse and found nothing at all reassuring in it. I walked around the corner of the house. There was the vine, tendrils still spreading over the southern wall, clusters of muscatel grapes peeping out through reddened leaves. They would be picked later, when the really cold weather came. But it was odd nevertheless to come upon them under this black and cloudy sky, with a fierce wind already chapping one's skin.

The courtyard was deserted. I had heard someone driving cattle out of it, and a few fresh cow pats remained as proof of their recent presence. There was no sign of life in the shack, but the old woman was almost certainly there, preparing the first meal of the day.

I looked up to the hills beyond, my eyes moving slowly across thickets of dwarf oaks, past the bare vineyard, up slope after slope where nothing grew but a carpet of close-cropped russet grass, like the hair on a bullock's flank. High above the *maquis*, on a distant shoulder of the hill, stood a truncated cone of grayish-brown stone blocks, so vast that their outline was easily distinguishable, even at this distance. This was the nuraghe—the Sardegra nuraghe, they called it—to which Mme. Enquist and Michael had climbed one stormy night during the summer. Beyond it, higher still, and bordered with clumps of stunted trees, the upland plateau known as the Giara de Lunas began. I thought, "It must be even colder up there than it is here."

That was where it had happened.

As I stood there watching the gnarled trees, bent now by the wind, and the great scudding clouds, yellowish-gray from the dust whirled through the air, I faced the fact that Ignazia had lied to me. Now I knew more than she did. Not that my knowledge could be of any conceivable value to a living soul. It was as useless as the toil of the anonymous builders who had sweated to raise those great piles of stone. The wind scoured my face and hands, buffeting me with a series of savage gusts that sounded like muted, distant thunder. I wanted to laugh, but the wind drove each explosion of laughter back into my open mouth, like so many wads of frozen cotton wool.

TODAY I find myself wondering whether it was not Zametti who started the whole thing, with those ambiguous remarks of his. Heaven knows what allusions Carl-Gustav could have read into them or how long they festered privately in his mind. I may even, in fact, have witnessed a long discussion between them on the subject, all concealed double meanings and unspoken implications. But at the time I was too blind—dazzled by the white heat of high summer—to see what was happening. Doubtless it is because of my suspicions that every time I recall that sensual and merciless radiance, I always associate it with the glowing shade, streaks of furnace-orange on a rose-pink ground, of the big beach umbrella and Professor Zametti's patrician features, like those of some worldly cardinal, bathed in the soft brightness that filtered through it.

I had studied under him at Rome University, as had Carl-Gustav before me. I spent an evening with him in Paris last September and found him incredibly little changed. Just how he manages to defy the passage of time in this way I have no idea. He has always been sober and moderate in his habits. Perhaps another contributory factor may be those regular weekly excursions into the Alps or Apennines in the company of one or two favorite students who had become personal friends —not to mention the passion he has for surrounding himself with young and preferably beautiful people. Zametti, now, is a *real* professor, a member of all the learned societies, delegate to every congress, and very often its president, and a great authority on neolithic culture in the Mediterranean—which may explain his attachment to Enquist at a time when the latter was still only a student.

But I suspect it was not young Enquist's academic achievements, remarkable as they were, that captivated the professor, so much as his masculine Nordic beauty and, somewhat later, the still more striking appearance of the woman he married. Zametti was no sentimentalist—he bore his wife's death with such perfect equanimity that it transcended the scandalous and became a joke. Nor had he an erotic side to his nature; I rather fancy that he gave up women fairly early in life, along with cigars. The only Eros he still cultivated was Plato's, the love of beauty per se: a purely visual love that perhaps, in moments of intimacy and among those men or women who were genuinely attached to him, might acquire a tactile dimension as well. In consequence his relationship with the Enquists spun itself a curious all-enveloping cocoon of tenderness and *amitié amoureuse,* though for all his sterling qualities he was neither their real friend, nor indeed capable of genuine affection. For him affection was simply one aspect of a purely abstract sensuality. He used to visit his Swedish friends regularly, much as some great bumble bee might return to its favorite flowers.

He belonged to an ancient family of mixed Neapolitan and Roman origin. The library walls in his modest house on the Via della Mercede were adorned with portraits of various ancestors, their armor inlaid with niello, their beards tapering over great starched ruffs. These gentlemen, despite their military appearance, had been for the most part in the banking business, as agents to Pope Sixtus V; and the prince who is the present head of the family still sits, in some capacity or other, on the boards of those banks that handle the Vatican's financial affairs.

The professor belonged to a cadet branch; he was actually a marquis, though he never used his title. In fact he voted Communist, and if I remember rightly, he may even have been a card-carrying party member. He had a fine Roman head, with a massive cranium and high straight forehead, a strong, fleshy nose, and beautiful brown eyes offset by a rather ugly mouth. His hair had been white ever since I had known him. He was inclined to stoutness and always dressed in light gray suits he had specially made for him in London. Surprisingly, he affected a French accent, rolling his *r*'s in an old-fashioned manner that was both elegant and slightly ridiculous—a distant echo of the *Ancien Régime*, I used to assume. This accent took on a particularly rich quality when the professor was quoting in ancient Greek.

He would sit there under the big beach umbrella, placidly fanning himself with a straw hat he never put on. Carl-Gustav was the soul of consideration where he was concerned. Every morning, when he came down to the beach, he brought the professor's umbrella and deck chair with him and took them back up again at midday. When they were folded, they looked as light as paper in his enormous hands. As I panted up those endless steps—the heat by then was almost incandescent —I found myself thinking that to carry the slightest object under this blazing sun would have been, for me, an intolerable burden. But Carl-Gustav was always ready to do anything he thought might please his guests. Such services on his part he seemed to regard as a matter of course. Indeed, his consideration reached such heights of unobtrusive perfection that one often failed to notice it. Late one evening, having noticed that I was out of cigars, he got up and disappeared for three-quarters of an hour, returning at last with a handful of those thin black local cheroots, mounted on a straw holder. Though it was pitch-dark, he had gone all the way down to the village and awakened the owner of the tavern by the Maddalena. He would not have dreamed of sending Pascal, who had been working all day in the fields and was now asleep; and Lupu would have flatly refused to go on such an errand after midnight.

"*Amante del sole,*" the professor was saying. The vowels rolled off his tongue with sensuous pleasure. He waved one soft, plump, half-open hand, as though in priestly benediction, toward the spot where Mme. Enquist lay stretched out on the sand. Her eyes were shut, but she was smiling. For the last moment or two Zametti had been singing her praises, and there was nothing she liked better than listening to conversation about herself—except perhaps sunbathing.

Carl-Gustav was lying on his back, on the other side of the deck chair. His powerful torso curved in a massive arch above his flat, heavily muscled stomach, rising and falling peacefully in time with the rhythm of his breathing. His eyes were closed

36

too, but the smile on his face had a different quality about it.

Without opening his eyes, he said, "There's this to say in favor of the sun as a lover. The relationship it maintains with its consorts is absolutely impersonal—like that of God with His creatures."

I caught the faintly nuanced tone of this remark, something unusual for Enquist. The fact that I still remember the phrase is proof enough that it struck me as peculiar at the time. But I did not understand, then, what lay behind it.

At that time Michael was a bony youngster on the verge of adolescence. His voice had just begun to break, but neither his cheeks nor his legs showed even the faintest trace of hair. All he had was a barely discernible fuzz of blond along his forearms. Neck bent as though beneath some invisible yoke, locks of hair falling over his eyes, he was energetically massaging Mme. Enquist's stomach. The expressionless set of his features, half-mulish, half-submissive, made him look like some little slave boy.

"Carl-Gustav is jealous of the sun," Mme. Enquist said, still smiling. "He's got good reason to be."

"Lucky sun, to be able to caress your body," Zametti exclaimed. "He is indeed your divine spouse; Carl-Gustav is no more than his representative here on earth. But even that is enough to make him universally envied."

I was only listening with half an ear. It was neither the sun nor Carl-Gustav that I envied, but Michael. She had such a lovely body that even now, more than ten years later, the memory of it tightens my throat and makes my mouth go dry.

37

Even the stomach that she made so outrageously coquettish a fuss about and that she was now having massaged, right under my nose, by Michael's small, thin, brown hands, had no more than softened with maturity, acquiring a delicate curve that deepened and enhanced the shape of her navel. And it was this wretched child, rather than myself, who had the privilege—indeed, the duty—of caressing it for hours at a time.

But in fact he did not caress it; he massaged it, very conscientiously, with slow, firm, relentless movements. He was doing a serious job. He really believed, since she told him so, that this exquisite stomach needed massaging.

I very much doubt that *she* thought so. The truth is that she was a tease, an *allumeuse*—a particularly lethal one at that, since she made a great show of being pure and cold and indeed *was* cold, if not pure. She never tired of proclaiming her astonishment at what dirty minds people had. She used to spend the whole summer in a two-piece bathing suit, ten years before anyone had even heard of the bikini. "What's wrong in that?" she kept asking. But at the time such a thing was unheard of, especially in this remote village, where she was the only one to exhibit herself so scantily clad. Foreigner, heretic—she took no notice of what the locals called her; they could please themselves. As far as she was concerned, she was quite at liberty to display her naked charms, either at home or in this secluded cove.

But the hills had eyes. Unseen herdsmen up in the *maquis*, their presence revealed only by the tinkle of goat bells; fishermen out in their boats, riding at anchor or sailing slowly around the rocky headland. They were not civilized, at least not in the sense that we are; they were not city dwellers or Scandinavians or Protestants. She knew this, but refused to take it into account. She was beautiful, wealthy, completely self-assured. Göteborg, that staid yet enchanting town, receives the foreign visitor with much hospitality, and welcomes exiles; but its inner circle of old families remains aloof and inaccessible. Mme. Enquist had been born and brought up there. Her family's name and wealth, the traditional respect Nordic peoples have for women, even her husband, if the need arose—all these had, throughout her life, formed a protective barrier between her and the outside world. She had never been afraid of anything. No one had ever taught her to feel fear. She had never learned the meaning of shame, or even of modesty. On the contrary, she felt that anything she did, anything she conceivably might do or say, was pure, natural, becoming, and without flaw.

Worse, she knew very well that this was not true. She was quite aware that the outside world was dominated by fear, shame, and taboos, and she enjoyed the sense of power she got from flouting them. At any given moment she was ready to defy convention, submit herself to trial by ordeal, simply to find out which of the two contestants, she or the world, would back down first and sublimely confident it would not be her.

Indeed, I have a strong suspicion that when Michael reached the age of puberty she put *him* to the test as well, quite naturally, without any scruple or hesitation, never for one moment realizing what she was doing. Why, for instance, did she not get her husband to massage her? There he was, two hundred-odd pounds of solid muscle, with big powerful hands that could satisfy any woman's need for sensual gratification. But no, it was not the pleasures of the flesh she needed so much as those of domination. What gave her so complete a hold over Carl-Gustav was, precisely, her indifference to him. And the little boy, a small resentful slave, toiled on in obedience to her will, eyes fixed and vacant.

Carl-Gustav lay there on the sand and did nothing. He was too civilized to rebel against this treatment, too highly educated to respect any taboos save those of good manners and scientific dogma, too inhibited to dare utter the word "impurity," too full of respect for his wife and too strong a character—he should have had a streak of weakness and femininity in him somewhere—to be able to bring her to her senses. He did not want to understand. He did not want to see the truth. He did not want to admit what he half-unconsciously knew already. Even if he had decided to act, he would have had no idea of how to go about it.

I realize that anything I say on this subject is liable to be prejudiced. Spiteful rancor is the prerogative of a spurned devotee—a category, I may add, into which all Mme. Enquist's devotees fell. Not that I was ever really in love with her. But there were times when she made me quite dizzy with desire. No one could look at that woman and not want her. Not content with displaying her charms too insistently, and with too little on, she was deliberately provocative. She stared at you in a come-hither way. The smile that accompanied these all too emphatic glances was overseductive, too consciously flirtatious. Do you see me? it announced. It's *you* I'm signaling. You're the only person here for me—and I'm the only person here for you.

There was nothing languorous or sensual about this gambit, no hint that she was actually offering herself to you. She was *there*, and that was all, a radiant presence laid on for your special benefit. The sole object of the operation was to dazzle you —and who could help being dazzled? She was the worst kind of *allumeuse*, elusive, untouchable, whose aim was to seduce you without compromising her own dignity by making the whole thing seem quite natural and innocent. What's more, she could do it without the slightest effort. Her line was never "Would you like to sleep with me?" but "Look at me; I'm the most beautiful and seductive woman you'll ever see in your whole life; they don't come any better." And it was true; no one could surpass her. Even far away in the big cities, the most you might find was someone to match her on equal terms; and here, in this harsh, burning wilderness, she had no rivals.

So now, with a sensual use of language that was not only Platonic but appropriate for a Platonist, Professor Zametti began to sing her praises. Perhaps describing her body was, for him, the equivalent of exploring it. Perhaps, too, he wanted to get back at Carl-Gustav, who after all had the privilege of touching it at any time. His verbal bouquets were accompanied by small, soft, circular movements of the hand, which fluttered through the burning air as though tracing out a miniature replica of Epicurus' intermundane space, that void where the gods dwell, blissful and superfluous, wholly indifferent to mankind.

"This life you lead, *carissima*," Zametti proclaimed with a greedy leer, "all this bright light and isolation, this love affair of yours with the sun, somehow endows you with perpetual virginity while leaving your functions as lover and mother intact."

Never pausing in his task, Michael, head still lowered, glanced up at Zametti when he said this. To be scrutinized from head to toe by those somber blue eyes, under their straight arching brows and high forehead, could—even then—be a disconcerting experience. More than once I found myself thinking what a devious expression the boy had. He struck me as stubborn, suspicious, and defiant. I know now that what produced this impression was, in fact, a mixture of obscure terror, unconscious despair, and above all the urge to rebel. He felt that he had his back to the wall, that he was thrown back on his last line of defense.

I REMEMBER this little scene now because Michael himself reminded his father of it in his letter. *I detested him,* he wrote. *To me he was just a dirty old man with a pot belly—an outsider who had nothing in common with the three of us, an intrusive alien who took the most presumptuous liberties with my mother, pawing her verbally, talking of her virginity and her sexual attributes, things that were as taboo to him as they were to me—and that I at any rate kept so, even in my imagination.*

He strongly disclaimed any suggestion of jealousy. *The proof of that,* he wrote, *is that I have never been jealous of you!* He reminded Carl-

Gustav of the summer all three of them had spent camping out in a tent above the beach while their recently bought house was still being put in order. Never, he said, would he forget those blazing sweltering afternoons—at two o'clock the heat and light were so intense they penetrated even the thick canvas of the tent—or the narrow slit through which the sky was visible, blue and shimmering, in sharp contrast to the stifling darkness inside. The light, he felt, was such that had it possessed eyes, it could have perceived the bee's larva, immured in its translucent cell within the honeycomb.

During one of these siestas, he recalled, Mme. Enquist had gone to sleep wearing nothing but the bottom part of her bathing suit. Carl-Gustav was lying close up against her, naked, eyes fixed on her face, one great hand exploring her nether belly under the triangular slip. *I am quite certain—as certain as though it were happening now—that I was not even disturbed by the sight.* He regarded it as entirely right and proper, part of the accepted order of things. Carl-Gustav was her husband, her lover; she was his wife, his lover too. Michael was conscious, in a perfectly happy and placid way, of being apart from them. *I did not envy you, any more than I would have envied the sun for being what it is.* Not only had he never been jealous of his father; he had never imagined them making love, much less spied on them. *In this last respect,* he wrote, *you have at least always maintained a quite exemplary discretion—but then, so have I, even in my thoughts!* In the margin Carl-Gustav had written: *You don't know why we were so discreet.*

It was true that Michael had never asked himself the reason for the striking contrast between all this naked exhibitionism and the total chastity of their relationship. He loved them, he believed in them, and that was enough. *I will even admit to you that at this moment, in the tent, I found my own naked, damp, undeveloped body beginning to throb with the first slow stirrings of passion. Yet I am quite certain that these symptoms of incipient virility had nothing to do with the spectacle before me. Though I found the sight of your conjoined bodies—bodies that were so much larger than mine—pleasing and harmonious, it never occurred to me to imagine them in still closer intimacy. Even now, when I am a grown man, it would cost me an effort to visualize your two bodies during intercourse, because my attachment is not to them but to you, to your unique essence as individuals. And precisely because it is you I am concerned with, and love, I find myself less able to approach your physical selves than I would the bodies of those who mean nothing to me.*

THIS, then, was the true meaning of the expression I had misread as devious stubbornness. It must have indicated either a total suppression of desire, springing from an inborn sense of propriety and universal order; or else a thorough and precocious assimilation of our civilization's taboos that rebelled against what Michael regarded as Zametti's lack of delicacy. But Carl-Gustav did no more than smile and register a token protest by means of several mildly ironical remarks. Yet each allusion Zametti made—if they *were* in fact allusions—every discreet barb planted in the wounds whose existence he *may* have sensed, sank slowly beneath the surface, and accumulated in the very depths of Carl-Gustav's being to form a purulent, festering core.

I am still not sure, despite everything, whether Zametti had any idea of what he was doing. He may even have delivered all those erudite, fantastic, and singularly pointless monologues just for his own amusement.

"Making your husband and son call you Freya shows a very sound instinct, *carissima*," he said. "You are too blond for a Mediterranean goddess—Venus, Aphrodite, Astarte, Isis, such names would be wholly inappropriate for you. Freya is the perfect choice. Carlo Gustavo, you have married *hominum divomque voluptas*. You will find her image everywhere from here to the Indus. To take an example near at hand, consider the Venus of Macomer or of Malta. Do you understand what such representations signify? Around the shores of the Mediterranean you will not find anything like your paleolithic images of Venus, with their sagging breasts and crudely steatopygous figures. Our goddess is both mother and lover, true, but in no way deformed by maternity. She is young and voluptuous, yet chaste as well. She is a divine being, inaccessible, untouchable. The gross mother figure of the Aurignacian period, poor creature, is tangibility personified. You can feel the artist's hands cupped around her bouncing and abundant flesh. Mediterranean man, on the other hand, trembles with a desire that can never be assuaged. He is paralyzed—and knows it—by the very intensity of his own adoration. His ardor is too intense, too vibrant with passion for any truly satisfying fulfillment. What we have here is Plato's Eros, the central characteristic of which is infinity—unending progress toward a never-to-be-achieved goal. Like waves forever surging in toward the shore they cannot reach. This is your true home, my dear Freya. If you were not so blond—not that I object, mark you; blondness as intense as yours quite dazzles us Mediterranean types—if you did not have hair of such amazingly pale gold, why I should swear you were born from this very sea and that when you claimed to have been swimming you had in reality just risen from the foam!"

As I listened to the professor's amiable inanities, against the muted roar of the surf, I found myself thinking that he had no idea how his beloved Astarte talked about *him*. Once, over the dinner table, I had heard her ask Carl-Gustav, with that clear, innocent laugh of hers, "Tell me, is it true what that woman told me in Rome? About Zametti having a reputation for rather *peculiar* tastes? I gather he has to wear a bowler hat when he's on the job—nothing else, she said—otherwise he can't make it!"

Nor was the professor aware that it was not Carl-Gustav who had chosen the name Freya. Mme. Enquist had in fact been baptized Marie-Dorotea-Ulrika, after her mother and her grandmothers. Carl-Gustav often called her Marie. But she insisted on being called Freya, not only by him but also, more surprisingly, by Michael. She had never let Michael refer to her as Mother or Mama. Some streak of Nordic—indeed, almost Wagnerian—

bad taste had driven her to masquerade under this symbolic name; it was about as preposterous as calling a Frenchwoman Venus.

Mme. Enquist was not in the least ashamed of her little flight of fancy, though it caused raised eyebrows among her fellow countrymen. It was only her non-Scandinavian friends, for whom the name had rather less precise significance, who called her by it and who asked Carl-Gustav for news of "Freya," in the belief that this would please him. They had no idea how irritating he found it. He was a highly civilized and fastidious person and could not help wincing at such histrionics on his wife's part. Yet he allowed her to pose as Freya for the benefit of her devotees—Freya, goddess from the Scandinavian pantheon, given a new lease of fashionable life by the bourgeoisie of the Romantic Age, complete with her whole ridiculous panoply: horned helmet, papier-mâché shield, and vast bosom crammed into a fish-scale cuirass.

The adoption of this ridiculous name, I feel, sheds less light on Mme. Enquist's character—she still arouses my passion, though I was never really in love with her—than the way she refused to let Michael call her Mama. To begin with I thought this refusal was simply one aspect of her determination not to grow old. I was wrong. She regarded herself as in love with her son. Carl-Gustav's letter to her contained the following passage: *In an old illustrated weekly I found a passage that you had underscored in red—the account, very poorly written, I may say, of a village crime, the farmer's wife who had been driven by jealousy to butcher her daughter-in-law with an ax. Here*

*were you, a wealthy young lady of good family,
sunbathing naked in Italy. Mother of a young son,
identifying yourself with this fifty-year-old peasant
woman in her old blue skirt and country bonnet,
even though you'd never so much as had a farm
tool in your hands since the day you were born!
Michael was only seven or eight at the time, yet
already you were rehearsing your role! I simply
cannot believe, even now, that you could have
taken yourself completely seriously at this early
stage.*

On the next line he had written just two words:
Quite crazy. But it should be borne in mind that
this "letter" to Freya was composed when he knew,
with final and absolute certainty, that she would
never read it. This fact lends a very special color
to his diagnosis.

AT THE same time Freya was instilling a sense of
respect into Michael, filling his head with the cult
of motherhood in general and of herself in particular. The only story she ever told him was one she
had gotten from a well-known sentimental ballad,
the story of the son who fell in love with a wicked
woman and was asked by her to produce a final,
unanswerable proof of his passion. What he must
do was bring her his mother's heart. So the boy
killed his mother, tore out her heart, and hurried
back with it to his mistress. But in his haste he
stumbled and fell on the way. The heart flew out
of his hand. As it hit the ground a voice came from
it, saying, "Have you hurt yourself, my son?"
Ever since the day when she first hurt me by

telling me this story, Michael wrote, *I have always retained a mental vision of the boy's handkerchief, a dirty gray or blue piece of material, gaping open, all spattered with blood, and of the heart itself lying there bleeding, by the dusty roadside. I can see it now. Since I had never been shown a real human heart, it looked like a big sheep's heart, oozing blood and befouled with dust.* He went on to complain bitterly about this traumatic childhood experience of his. *Was she justified, I ask myself, in deliberately exposing me, at this very early age, to something that had so deep and lasting an effect on me? Not to mention the way she refused to be called Mother and would accept no role save that of the young woman who was my friend and equal. Mark that I do not say "goddess." I detest the way that horrible old creature Zametti will keep buttering her up with his syrupy mythological flights of fancy every time he visits us. For me she has always been identified with that bleeding heart and the low, tender, anxious voice saying, "Have you hurt yourself, my son?"—to such a degree, indeed, that despite her passion for nakedness, despite the beauty of her body, which I saw daily and even now retains all its perfection, I have always kept our relationship within the bounds of propriety, even in my dreams.*

And to convince Carl-Gustav of his innocence in this respect, he described the one incestuous dream that he, in common with most adolescents, had experienced. Significantly, Freya remained invisible throughout. Between his lusting flesh and her there suddenly appeared a square of thick cardboard, roughly hacked out with a knife— *and as you know,* he wrote, *I have always hated the*

*scraping sound of a knife as it cuts through card-
board; it gives me goose pimples and sets my teeth
on edge.* He transfixed the cardboard, and instantly
the dream faded. But already all awareness of the
body that tempted him to commit incest had been
obliterated from his mind. All that remained, for
one brief fraction of a second, was the ludicrous
spectacle of this cardboard collar impaled on his
person.

Personally I have no doubt whatsoever as to
the innocence of Michael's intentions. Indeed, the
whole situation is by no means hard to analyze.
We can all be read as easily as a book—in retrospect. But our future remains as unpredictable as
ever. The specter of uncertainty looms in us and
around us. Why did Michael protest his innocence
so emphatically? Why employ the solemn word
"innocence" at all? These feverish and argumenta-
tive assertions were all part of his desperate defense against Freya's irresistible invasion of his
personality. If she had not marked him with the
seal of physical incest, his agonized refusal of her
advances had nevertheless damaged him almost as
badly. It is just possible, on the other hand, that
no such advances ever took place. All the evidence
at my disposal can be interpreted in at least two
different ways, each of which directly contradicts
the other.

IN THE same way, it may be conceded that any of
Professor Zametti's remarks, taken in isolation,
prove nothing beyond the fact that he was an old
hand at this charming if pedantic brand of whim-

sicality. But I am rather sure the habit also allowed him to direct shafts of malicious mockery at his friend—his friends, rather, all three of them—or even to suggest to them—but no, I'm going too far, that's out of the question. His age and experience make it very likely that he did, in fact, understand the situation; but at the very most I think he got a mischievous pleasure from half-revealing it to the protagonists, by indirect and erudite allusions. It is possible, but I shall never know for certain. If I were to ask him point-blank, I have no doubt that he would raise his arms in scandalized denial. And yet . . .

"Tell me," he inquired, "why didn't you settle on Malta? Melita, as the island used to be called—its still more ancient name, Delphine, embodies the archaic word for the uterus—was beyond any doubt the main center of some feminine cult. Think of all those goddesses and priestesses and the statues of women sleeping on their sides, no doubt awaiting some prophetic dream! And what about the underground shrines at Hal Saflièni, those grottoes cut from the living rock that still show traces of the red paint that once covered them? What do they represent but a descent to the earth-mother? What are they if not symbols of life within the womb? It is there, my dear Freya, that you should have revealed yourself to us!"

Carl-Gustav said, "I find those caves very tedious. Nothing but dust, bad air, silence, and claustrophobia."

"Be honest, Carlo Gustavo. The reason you picked Sardinia, despite its unfriendly atmosphere, is because this island lies under the aegis of the Father. You wanted to play a joke on the feminine

51

principle. He really hates you, *carissima*, in his tender loving way. He chose this land of Saturn as a secret act of defiance against you. The god of the ancient Sardinians, you know, Sardus Pater, was identical not only with the Carthaginian deity Baal-Moloch, that devourer of young children, but also with Saturn, who used to swallow his own offspring!"

"You know as well as I do that the cathedral of Cagliari is dedicated *Sanctae Mariae Reginae Sardorum*," said Carl-Gustav.

"Camouflage, mere camouflage! Look at all the little bronze images my excellent and learned friend Illiu and his pupils have collected. Nothing but fierce armed warriors, and those shepherds, dear me, with such short tunics that they reveal what should more properly be hidden, and above all the flute player found at Ittiri, whose pipes are identical with the *launeddas* still used by present-day herdsmen and who is depicted in a, hmm, *prominent* physical condition not normally associated with *musical* performance—"

Freya was laughing by now, clear innocent peals of mirth that assorted oddly with both the professor's salacious remarks and the statuette in question, which we all knew.

With a touch of irritation in his voice Carl-Gustav said, "What connection is there between these masculine figurines, obscene or otherwise, and your theory that Sardinia is only dedicated to the Virgin to conceal its true underlying allegiance?"

"My point is that you can trace the Virgin back as far as your neolithic idols—that's the origin of the Mater Dolorosa, with her child on her knees.

52

Think of the statues of Sa Domu è S'Orcu, or Santa Vittoria de Serri—they still represent the eternal *madre mediterranea*, but always in her aspect as mourner. What we see is Cybele weeping for Attis, Venus and Adonis, Ishtar and Tammuz, mother and lover in one, keening in sorrow over the young vegetation god—"

"Venus was *not* the mother of Adonis," said Carl-Gustav. A streak of genuine annoyance was beginning to show through his normal affable manner. "Nor, if it comes to that, was Cybele the mother of Attis, nor—"

"But they all share a common genesis if you look back far enough, for heaven's sake." By now the professor was well away, enthralled by his own argument. "I hardly need to remind you, my dear fellow, that what we are concerned with, invariably, is the basic Isis-Osiris relationship—the mythical expression of a fundamental complex too well known to need identification. Think of the way the Egyptians represented it: Isis as Queen of Heaven, with Night arching over her arms and legs, the vault of darkness, correct? Her small, brown, pointed breasts are hanging over the body of Osiris. He is dead, but his resurrection is assured; he lies there in the passive attitude betokening death, but he is nevertheless in a state of erection. Here we have man, the earth, pointing upwards towards the starry feminine firmament, symbol of both marriage and motherhood, forever desirable, forever out of reach. Each one of us, dear Freya, is his mother's son. This myth was invented by sons. Mothers seek only to exist and to create their sons. And the passion engendered in these sons—spiritual rather than physical passion, but are not the two things indistinguishable?—has produced the story of Isis mourning the death of Osiris, who had been her lover. You will find the same cult from one end of the Mediterranean to the other. Everywhere the bull plays the same part in it, that of the sacrificed son, immolated by man in his role as husband and father, done to death by a blatantly sexual sword thrust—"

"Really, now, professor!" Carl-Gustav exclaimed. His tone was meant to indicate mock alarm but merely succeeded in conveying embarrassment. Michael said not a word, but went on massaging his mother.

Zametti, however, was enjoying himself too much to brook any interruption.

"But if the ritual sacrifice of the son, whether in person or through the substitution of the lunar-horned bull, is accepted without a murmur wherever the great mother-lover reigns supreme, from Crete to Spain, the situation is quite different in those regions dominated by the father—that is, in the lowest depths of the subconscious. Here all concord ceases, together with that tender acquiescence in the obsidian knife drawn across the filial victim's throat, to be replaced by a merciless struggle between father and sons. Pater Sardus, or, if you prefer it, Baal—that is to say, Saturn—devours them. But then they rise in revolt and castrate him. The father *has* to eat his children; if he does not, they will rob him of his virility. You will recall, my dear Carlo Gustavo, the tradition—it must be at least as old as Timaeus—according to which the ancient Sardinians used to take their fathers, when aged and impotent, to the edge of a precipice and throw them off it—laughing heartily as they did so, in a way that surely merits the epithet *sardonic.*"

I raised myself on one elbow. Michael had neither changed his attitude nor stopped what he was doing, but his eyes were now fixed on the professor. Carl-Gustav had rolled over on his stomach again. Eyes closed, cheek resting against the hot sand, he murmured, "You know what Polybius thought of that gossip monger Timaeus—and modern historiography has found no occasion to revise his judgment."

"Timaeus as a source is worthless, I agree," the professor said, and then added triumphantly, "but until the beginning of the last century Sardinia maintained the tradition of the *accabadores*—the dispatchers, you might call them. They were old village women who could be summoned at need, like keeners or midwives. They were only called out when some member of the family was taking too long to die. They would turn up in the middle of the night, and then, with a firm and charitable hand, slit the dying man's throat or split his skull with a chopper, and all in the name of the Father. But whatever you do, don't refer to this practice when there are any Sardinians present—it makes them very angry indeed. They maintained the whole thing's a lot of slanderous rubbish. Nothing like that ever happened here, they say."

Then he launched into a semi-Voltairean, semi-ethnological disquisition on the cult of the Virgin. According to him, every red-blooded Mediterranean male was in love with her.

"Above all, those who still practice the *taurobolium*—don't you see, the bull is the son, the son is the bull—now, what was I saying, my friends? Ah

55

yes. Above all, those who still keep up the tradition of killing bulls in a ritual manner—even when they blaspheme against her, it is her purity and sacrosanctness they deny, in contrast to the French or the Germans, whose oaths are directed against God, or hell, or damnation, or the sacraments of the Church. For us, on the other hand, all these things are united in her—which means in *you, carissima!*"

He then went on, with obvious pleasure, to emphasize that the complete décolleté of the Cretan mother goddess was partially preserved in representations of the Madonna nursing her divine child.

"For thousands of years the same passionate yet restrained eroticism has continued to manifest itself, symbolized by this adoration of virgin, bride, and young mother in one divine being, whom artists have endowed with the same physical charms—radiant, yet at the same time a torment because so patently unattainable—that we find in archaic images. Archaic—now what was I saying? Archaic—ah, yes, that's right, *the smile.* I feel quite sure you would find it on the Venus of Macomer's face, if only the vicissitudes of time hadn't left her without a head. The divine smile, just as one might imagine it on the face of the goddess herself—always supposing she had human features or indeed any physical existence—while contemplating her creatures and what she has made of them. Or, to put it another way, while contemplating herself and the sufferings that—for her own inscrutable reasons and purposes—she chooses to undergo. A complex half-smile, serene, satisfied, impenetrable, and, above all, of quite remarkable inanity. Are we going to have lunch soon?"

I hardly heard his peroration; I was far more preoccupied by the way Michael was looking at him, with the dark, lowering scowl of some young bull about to charge. Carl-Gustav made no reply, and I did not bother to look at him; I assumed he had simply become bored with the argument and was relaxing in the sun, imperturbable as ever. I was quite wrong—wrong about all of them, in fact, except Freya herself, who now observed coquettishly, "So that's why you chose Sardinia rather than Malta, is it? To get away from me."

"Who could ever escape you?" Carl-Gustav murmured. "I would not even dare to consider the possibility. I am irretrievably lost. Delivered, sold, betrayed."

"Betrayed?" she repeated, somewhat put out. "By whom?"

"What I mean is that I am a slave. You know that perfectly well. *Your* slave."

"It doesn't sound like that to me. A very resentful, rebellious sort of slave, I'd have thought."

"Not true," he said softly, "not true." And then, "The professor's right, it's time for lunch. Let's go."

SO CARL-GUSTAV did not react in any visible fashion to Zametti's subtle insinuations. Even more surprising was the absence of any reaction on Freya's part after the incident at the Funtana Cuperta. Yet this was the first distant forerunner of the *avvenimenti* that took place twelve or thirteen years later.

57

The Funtana Cuperta, which was located on Enquist's estate, had been built by the ancient Sardinians, in all likelihood for some ritual purpose. The spring itself was underground, and to reach it one went down about twenty steps beneath the surface. Outside was the ravine, thickly overgrown with scrub and bushes, hazel in particular. Once I had cut a few hazel sticks here to make bows for Michael; but I knew little about such things and picked them far too green, so the arrows they discharged flew only a few feet. The lower end of the ravine emerged between the houses close to the Maddalena; its upper extremity reached the edge of the plateau. These dark, lush thickets filled the air with a pleasant aromatic scent and were full of butterflies, dragonflies, and loud-buzzing bluebottles. Here and there a tree rose above the shrubbery. Higher still was the blue sky and the wind and a descant of birdsong.

But down by the pool, below ground, where those heavy stone steps descended between two Cyclopean walls, all was dim and dank and silent. The roof was made from blocks of stone set exactly parallel to the stairway and similarly stepped, so that it followed one down into the chill-damp darkness. Right at the bottom, a square of still, black, ice-cold water gleamed among the shadows. The peasants very seldom used it, not so much out of superstitious dread at its silent, secretive atmosphere, its air of darkness at noon, as from plain laziness. It meant too long a walk; they preferred to draw their water from the Funtana de Janas. Yet in the old days it must certainly have been a cult shrine, a place imbued with holy awe. Its symbolism was obvious—the mother, the teeming earth, life-giving water, a hole through which generation was accomplished. But nobody thought of such things any longer.

One morning in late spring, Michael and his mother were walking back from the village together. He was still a very small boy and had to hold on to Freya's hand to keep up with her. When he described the incident in the letter he wrote his father, he could offer no explanation either of how they came to be near the Funtana Cuperta or what they were doing there. All he could remember was the scene itself: the big peasant woman, standing with her full pitcher beside the fountain, who suddenly stopped Freya and began shouting insults at her.

I have seen so many women of her sort that I can easily picture what she looked like: a squat, dumpy creature, thin-lipped, yellow-complexioned, with a sharp aquiline nose and glinting eyes, awkwardly bundled up in her black shawl, great gourdlike breasts straining under a dirty gray blouse, black skirt bunched over ample buttocks—a plump mother hen except for the head, which, unexpectedly, was that of some bird of prey.

There she stood, spitting insults in Freya Enquist's face or, to be more accurate, telling her a number of unpleasant truths. Michael understood only a part of what she was saying, since she spoke in patois; but it was enough to shock him to the core. He raised his head and looked up at his mother, and his feeling of shock became even more intense when he saw how utterly unmoved she was. There she stood, her radiantly beautiful countenance poised above the light short-sleeved dress she was wearing, arms bare and white, a goddess indeed. Her expression had changed not at all; she did not so much as blink or raise an eyebrow, but calmly surveyed her assailant. The woman was upbraiding her in a raucous, strident voice, for showing *sa carre*. She did not use the Italian equivalent, *la carne*, but said *sa carre*, which is Sardinian dialect. Since the Sardinians are both chaste-living and coarse-spoken, their use of this phrase, literally "the flesh," was restricted to a specific and obscene connotation, which the village woman now reinforced by adding *su sessu* and *su cunnu*. All this she bawled out at the top of her voice, accusing Freya of being a bitch in heat, of having *su male crabinu*, the goat's disease; she even called her *bagassa*, a common whore.

As Michael admitted to his father, the shock he got from the insults themselves was not nearly so great as that produced by Freya's incomprehensible silence. Then the old woman broke off, as abruptly as she had began. A moment before the incident Michael had been trudging up those interminable steps in peaceful silence. Now, a moment after it, he was doing so once more, just as if nothing had happened.

Freya never breathed a word of this encounter to Carl-Gustav. Nor did she ever discuss it with her son; he might just as well have been an idiot deaf mute as far as she was concerned. It really looks as if she never gave the matter another moment's thought, had no urge, even temporarily, to leave the district where such a thing could happen to her, and did not for one second consider altering her own habits. She was above and beyond all such reactions, isolated within herself, protected by her family's adoration. But her greatest shield against reality was her narcissism, her pride, her inability to feel fear, her flat refusal to submit her will to anything or anybody—much less the taboos of the village or social restrictions as such.

It is quite true that she was unapproachable and, in her own way, possessed of sovereign power. I am not emulating Zametti's deplorable weakness for mythological speculation when I say this. I merely record the impression she made. I am even ready to admit—as a means of allaying any fear that I might still be under her spell—that all these characteristics of hers may have been no more than a testament to her innate stupidity. But I *knew* her; the phenomenon existed and who cared how or why? This was the way she was, and that was that.

THE SECOND bad omen—there were no others —was Don Efisio's final visit. Don Efisio was the village priest, predecessor of the present incumbent, Don Pantaleo. He climbed up to the Enquists' house one day, panting and sweating, mopping off his face with a big checkered handkerchief. He was a short, stocky, down-to-earth figure, and his big head, still with more black hair than gray, could have belonged to a shepherd up on the Giara. The women crowded around him, kissing his hand and calling him *babbaï*, like children. He endured their attentions uncomplainingly and with considerable dignity. Then he turned toward the Enquists' house and asked if the *professore* was in.

Carl-Gustav had just come out and now stood at one corner of the terrace, watching Don Efisio's reception by the peasant women. His expression was of solemn amusement. At the far side of the courtyard, beside the stable door, stood Lupu Marteddu, motionless, eyes taking in everything and everyone. Carl-Gustav walked a few steps forward to meet the priest, greeted him, and took him off to his study. This was an all-white room but still very dim and shady after the glare of the midday sun. It contained nothing but rows of bookshelves, a big table-topped desk, two chairs, and a shotgun propped up against one corner of the wall.

In his pseudoletter to Freya, Carl-Gustav described this visit from the priest with an almost insane wealth of comic detail. Apparently the two men sat in silence until Assunta appeared, carrying a tray with two glasses and a carafe of Moscato. Then Carl-Gustav offered Don Efisio a cigar, which was politely refused. They both hesitated a moment before speaking, Carl-Gustav in an attitude of well-bred patience, Don Efisio frowning and worried. In other circumstances this discussion with a priest who was himself half-peasant would doubtless have begun with an exchange of rural small talk about the weather, the crops, and the latest local news. But the people in these parts were sparing of words and too proud to approach any topic obliquely. A wasp was buzzing against the window pane; the closed Venetian blinds laid zebra stripes of light and shade on the glass. Presently the wasp advanced into the room, as though riding down a long ray of sunlight. Carl-Gustav, who was beginning to feel bored, followed its progress with one eye.

At last Don Efisio made up his mind and began to speak, slowly, painfully, and with visible reluctance. It was not his business, he said, to lay down rules of conduct for the *professore*, who did not belong to the Holy Roman Church and was also a scholar, a far more learned scholar than himself. But it was his bounden duty, as a Christian and as the *pàrroco* of the village, to explain to the Enquists, *gente molto dabbene*, most respectable people, who that is to say—

Don Efisio began to mop his face again. He was sweating profusely. He knew very well, he went on, that fashions were changing. He himself had no objection, personally, to what people did nowadays. On the other hand, he was responsible for the souls of the fishermen and laborers in his flock. It was them he was concerned about at present. He felt quite sure that the *signora*, who was also a person of education and learning, had no bad intentions whatsoever. In Sweden, it was undoubtedly the custom to, ah—well, the long and short of it was, different countries had different customs, and so on. Here, certainly it was *not* the custom. Here it was something quite unheard of. In big towns like Sassari and Cagliari, where the tourists came to spend their holidays, no one found it surprising. But here it was quite another matter. What could one expect in such a place? The people were *gente pòvera*, peasants, shepherds. They didn't understand. He, Don Efisio, had no wish to inflict his advice on anybody—but if the *signora* could perhaps be persuaded to wear a bathing suit that was more, er, that is to say *less*—anyway, a costume of the kind most people wore—

He left his speech unfinished. His eyes, black points set in yellowish whites, were watching Carl-Gustav steadily. Their resolute expression declared, in plain terms, what Don Efisio's discreet circumlocutions had no more than hinted at. *If you do not agree*, they said, *you and I will never see one another again*. The prospect gave Carl-Gustav a twinge of regret. Don Efisio had few intellectual pretensions, but Carl-Gustav nevertheless found him a decent, simple man, for whom he felt both respect and affection.

"I hardly need remind you, Don Efisio, of what our Lord said. That it is not from without but within ourselves that there come—"

"—*luxuria, nequitia, malae cogitationes*," the priest murmured, with unruffled amiability. "I know, I know, *onorato professore*. I said as much to you myself, a moment ago. I am well aware that the *signora* has no bad intentions. She does not speak to anyone, and in particular not to men. She is your wife and I respect her. But please try to understand that it is not her I am concerned about, so much as my poor ignorant malice-ridden peasants. *They* are the ones with evil thoughts. Not that they would ever touch a hair of the *signora's* head. In these parts attacks on women or girls are quite unheard of, even up on the Giara or among the mountain shepherds. Such things simply never happen. The occasional murder, perhaps—but not here, quite definitely not here. Nothing's ever happened around our district. In other parts of the island, maybe—Gallura, say, or Logudoro—but not often, and always as a matter of honor. It is their honor that forces them to kill. They're not entirely to blame; they're unlucky victims, *pòveri sventurati*. When the situation comes up, they're obliged to avenge the insult—there's nothing else they can do. Otherwise they have to leave town for good. But if they *do* avenge their honor, it comes to much the same thing. They still have to go into hiding for years. In certain villages you'll find scarcely a man left. But there's nothing like that goes on here. Life is uneventful. The soil is poor, and work correspondingly hard. I don't need to tell you *that*, though, seeing that you're"—and here the priest, straining his dignity to its limits, descended, whether out of kindness or a Christian sense of duty, to a plain lie—"seeing that you're as good as one of us." Carl-Gustav found this gesture very touching.

But its main object was to persuade him, to make him bow before local custom. Don Efisio knew, and knew that Carl-Gustav knew, that to be "one of us" meant having been born here. Nothing else would do. Indeed, for the upland folk even the village fishermen were no better than foreigners, to be excluded from the clan, now and always.

"It's the women who are causing most trouble," Don Efisio went on. "Not that they've complained, oh, dear me, no. But I know they harbor evil thoughts. They repent, I give them a penance, and they accept it. They are equally well aware that no one is doing anything wrong, or even intending to. It's just the occasional word that gets dropped here and there. Sometimes people make a joke of it, too. You know what their menfolk are like, *gente cattiva*, coarse ignorant brutes. Oh, they feel thor-

65

oughly ashamed of themselves afterwards: they don't like talking about such things. But the women know. They say to me: 'Babbaï, we can't help ourselves. The evil thoughts are too strong for us. I've been having them again. I'm sorry, Father, I'm repentant, but they just won't go away.' Do you understand?"

His eyes searched Carl-Gustav's face. But the truth was that Carl-Gustav would never, in any circumstances, have considered taking the matter up with his wife. He was too proud, too proud of her, too much in love. From the very first word Don Efisio uttered, he had guessed what was up and had made his decision to stand firm. Hence that small stab of regret when he felt he was losing poor Don Efisio's friendship. Here was a man he not only respected but admired, and now he would have to forgo his company. He smiled amiably and said, "You know better than I do, Don Efisio, what Christ commanded us: *Judge not, that we be not judged*. And who will cast the first stone?"

Yes, it's true, my poor Marie, he wrote, *I actually said those words. Without realizing their implication. Never thinking that I was insulting you unawares, since in the Gospel the person concerned is a prostitute. You, a prostitute! Forgive me, my poor darling. They sell their bodies for money, whereas you offered everyone the sight of yours, free and gratis: a far more charitable attitude than theirs—and much worse, too.*

The priest did not so much as blink. He said, "Every place has its own customs, and men must respect them. All humanity follows the same pattern. Only Jesus is different. We try to live according to His commandments, but we are too feeble."

66

He continued to stare at Carl-Gustav, with a dull, bemused expression. This meant merely that he was thinking hard. At last he found the words he was searching for.

"If the *signora* would deign to conform out of charity, perhaps—or humility—"

"She is very far from humble," Carl-Gustav said, laughing. "I wouldn't even dare mention the subject to her."

Don Efisio scrutinized him in silence for a long moment. Then he said, with regret, "You are a proud man yourself, *professore*. Too proud." He shook his head, disconsolate. In a slow voice, as though to himself, he murmured, "You are wealthy, intelligent, and good-looking. But these poor peasants are ignorant wretches who have nothing, absolutely nothing."

He shrugged and hauled himself ponderously to his feet. "Well, I've said what I came to say. Forgive me. I was only trying to help. My respects to the *signora*."

He went out, received the salutations of Pascal and the women with his habitual gravity—Lupu was no longer to be seen—and made his way down the sunken road, dusty foliage shading him overhead. In order to negotiate the stone steps with greater ease, he hoisted up the skirts of his soutane in both hands as he walked.

And yet, my love, you knew very well they used to watch you from a distance, lying flat on their stomachs in the undergrowth. You knew that here, in this solitude, there is always somebody watching every move you make. You also knew that they had no real intentions or desires; they simply wanted to look at you—but from the first moment you were revealed to them, their own wives were transformed into wretched scarecrows, mere humble beasts of burden. Even here you had to have this shabby little triumph, just as you had to have all the others back home. He went on with a plethora of obscure allusions to various rows and scandals they had had in Uppsala and Stockholm. I did not realize then that certain eccentricities on Freya's part—I still have no idea what they were— had been responsible for their leaving the country in the first place.

YET THIS had not been the only, or indeed the main, factor behind their withdrawal to a remote and poverty-stricken Sardinian village. It was, of course, Freya's pride, constantly hungry for fresh feminine triumphs—triumphs barren and remote, in which no bedazzled lover ever participated— that finally made the whole project impossible. But there was something else involved: Carl-Gustav's passion for her. *I wanted to be alone with you,* he wrote. *I wanted the two of us to form an island, here in this secluded house, itself one island within another. But it was you who stood at the heart of this threefold isolation, in eternal and unapproachable solitude. Why did you not warn me in time? Why could you not have rejected me from the beginning? Had you no pity, no common human kindness? You must have recognized your own indifference to my fate, your inability to want me, or indeed anyone. You never felt desire for a man—except once, and then it was too late, and you too found yourself struggling to grasp the un-*

attainable. Enough to make one die laughing, isn't it? I feel this wave of hysterical laughter surge up in me—but now it can never find utterance. Not any more. My poor pillar of salt.

The tone of these ramblings was oddly tender and emotional, charged with angry pity, a kind of hard-hearted compassion. At the beginning, though, he had been in thrall to something quite different: an ungovernable physical passion. Any man capable of such an obsession would have felt this way about Freya Enquist. When I first knew her she was about thirty; and even ten or a dozen years later, I would still have been ready to go quite wild over her had she ever given me the slightest encouragement.

This makes it all the easier for me to understand Carl-Gustav's behavior, and I hardly need to say that his hints of torrid desire came as no great surprise to me. What *did* take me aback was the un-looked-for revelation of just how unrequited this passion had been. I was very young at the time and never thought of asking myself—as well I might have done—whether Freya was not in fact completely frigid. Now I am sure she was. The burning, bitter reproaches Carl-Gustav flung at her on paper—too late and to no useful purpose—brought a flush to my cheeks as I read them. I never felt ashamed of my indiscretion in reading Michael's farewell letter; but one or two intimate sections of his father's barely decipherable scrawl gave me moments of acute embarrassment. Poor Michael was chaste enough, but here there was no lack of *luxuria, nequitia,* and *malae cogitationes.*

He had prostrated himself before her and on her. He had really groveled in frustration while

69

covering that great white body, searching for the dry and unresponsive mouth that opened so reluctantly to his kisses, the exquisite tongue that stirred so seldom and with such obvious lack of enjoyment. *Whenever I made love to you,* he wrote, *you would keep staring fixedly at my face.* His words straggled, and splutters of ink showed where a sudden heavy pressure of the hand had splayed the nib. *Those great eyes of yours, only two or three inches beneath mine, yet so blank and dark. Your mind was miles away. You just went on staring, as if you were trying to find out just how completely I could lose all semblance of humanity—writhing as though in an epileptic seizure, cretinized by the violence of my passion, that passion you never shared and you neither could nor would understand!*

He had never bothered to stop and ask himself whether Freya's inability to comprehend sexual desire might not have caused *her* suffering. Was it not possible that she felt such shame and guilt about her frigidity that she *had* to reassure herself by means of physical exhibitionism? The question never crossed his mind. He had never been capable of feeling sorry for her. He was a handsome man, with considerable charm, and strongly sensual in his own discreet fashion. In his youth he had made numerous conquests. *All the women I ever made love to were happy, satisfied, and grateful. They all became genuinely fond of me, right from the very first time we spent together. I was initiated at the age of sixteen, by a little prostitute. She was so satisfied (or touched by my innocence) that she refused to take my money. As I was with a school friend, she wouldn't let him have her, but excused herself on the grounds that she was "tired." The boy bore a grudge against me for the next couple of months. Even now, I know I could satisfy any other woman—but not you, the only one I want to satisfy.*

Not content with this, you keep me on a chain, like a prisoner. Oh, you tell me you appreciate me, you like me, you wouldn't want to break up our marriage. But the word "like," as used by you, simply means that you don't actively dislike me, that I don't offend your sight—no more than that. It's as though you were discussing a fine dog that you felt particular liking and affection for. There is never the slightest sexual element in anything you do or say. Note that I do not add "or in any of your reactions," because you have none. No, that's not entirely true. You like it when I stroke your back very gently or blow in your hair. It's the nearest you can ever get to sensuality—and it's just not enough, my poor child.

For now, at last, he had succeeded in bringing himself to pity her, through the employment of that extreme sanction that remains known only to Lupu and myself. But the most extraordinary thing was the way Carl-Gustav addressed Freya in the present tense, as though she were there before him, among the empty bottles that littered the floor of his room. He recalled every detail of their life together—first meetings, engagements, honeymoon. This last had left him half-crazy with frustrated passion, yet still nursing the hope that one day he might make contact with her through that tender, heartbreaking, totally chaste body of hers. Yet "chaste" is not quite the right epithet, since it implies at least the possibility of its opposite; "absent" would be nearer the mark. A sleeping body, with the nullity of a vegetable or a flower.

I only saw you those two or three nights at the beginning—eyes shut, head thrown back, lips half-parted and trying just to brush mine, the merest touch, no more. Your body did seem to respond in a way when we came together—but only for a short while. Why did these physical reactions of yours lessen every night, so swiftly that a week or two later there was no trace of them left? What had happened? Looking back, I am convinced that this was not the real you, but simply an echo of what that bastard Eklundh taught you. He had the right idea. Make you and let you go, without the slightest effort to hang on to you.

Eklundh is a common enough name in Sweden, but to spell it with that final *h* is a trifle pretentious. The person in question was, I gather, a baritone at the Royal Opera House in Stockholm—a short, ugly, vigorous man, bursting with health and energy, quite intelligent for a professional singer and far too sensible to fall in love with Freya. He had been her first and last-but-one lover; and she had shattered Carl-Gustav by describing the whole affair to him, with an excessive wealth of cold and clinical detail.

You told me, Carl-Gustav wrote, *that if you were to meet him in the street today you would not recognize him. You would ask yourself what his name was and where you had met previously. Yet you also admitted that you had been in love with him and explained just how you responded to the various lubricious acts he initiated—though if I tried the same sort of thing I would meet with a* stony refusal. "But you're different," you used to tell me, "I love you." I remember your saying one night, "Look, he's a head shorter than you are and about twice as thick around the waist; he's just an ugly, pot-bellied little man. And you're a damned sight more virile than he is—I should know, I've handled both of you!" Nothing could have better demonstrated your insensitivity than this monstrously vulgar attitude, so down-to-earth that it was guaranteed to freeze any lesser passion than mine on the spot. You sickened me—and yet I loved you more than ever! But if I took your hand and brought it anywhere near my body, your fingers would stiffen, as though at the approach of some disagreeable and dangerous object, and your palm would go flat and hard and hostile. Resistance; flat refusal. After that you never wanted anything. "The only emotion the male sexual organ arouses in me is one of repulsion," you used to say, very brisk and positive, as though stating a scientific fact. I apologize for possessing so disgraceful a stigma. I beg your pardon, as I have so often done in the past, for finding this morsel of flesh essential to any experience of pleasure. It interested you no more than did the pleasure it generated, which you never found comprehensible, much less an object of desire. I inflicted my flesh upon you, and you writhed in disgust and embarrassment; I might have been some torturer with a branding iron. The only sound you ever uttered was a whimper of agony, at that throbbing, distending penetration you could never see any purpose in and to which you only submitted out of unhappy consideration for my needs. I ought to have escaped long ago. I should have left you right at the beginning, the first time you patted the shoulder above your face in that amiable way you had—so full of pitying condescension, that gesture, just the way one pats an animal after it's run a good race or done some tough work, while it's still panting to get its breath back, head down, absolutely done in, some big, stupid, gentle beast of burden. "I want you to get some benefit from me," you used to tell me, in the bounty of your heart, without ever realizing the shame and humiliation such an attitude produced. You were the understanding nurse, making sympathetic allowances for this filthy priapic creature, this great beast panting and thrusting, muzzle buried in the pillow.

Yet I had no eccentric needs. I neither indulged in fantasies nor made excessive demands on you. My only fault was to be a young and virile man, very much in love and brimming over with physical passion. That coarse greaseball Eklundh had the right idea—just one more scalp for his collection, a few brief meetings, straight into bed, straight on the job, see you some time, darling, and on to the next one! But you made out it was all quite different with me. You did me the honor of loving me, of restraining your feelings where I was concerned. You gave me nothing you had permitted Eklundh. It had all been such a repulsive disappointment that you let three years go by between your initiation and the love—of a sort— you conceived for me. I am even prepared to believe that you really do love me in your own sexless, passive fashion, that this is the only love you have to offer—or was, until very recently. It's an ironic joke, isn't it, darling? An appropriate punishment,

*too; you're hit just where you wounded me your-
self. Now it's your turn to face a total refusal, my
poor oh-so-tender goddess—and to endure the
same total frustration.*

Then he went on to describe scenes she had
known nothing of. One particular winter night, for
example, at a time when it was dark from early
afternoon till the middle of the following morning
and Carl-Gustav had lain awake hour after hour,
crucified by unsatisfied and insatiable desire. The
house was still, no lights were on, and outside the
snow lay deep and silent. There was a faint pale
glow along the road, thrown up by the reflection
of the street lamps in the snow; this half-light
dimly revealed Freya's blond head lying on the
pillow, eyes closed, mouth set in a delectably childish pout. He brushed her sleeping, nonsentient lips
with his, tried to part them with the tip of his
tongue. She turned her head away and wiped her
mouth with the back of her hand, a small, precise
gesture. She had not even awakened. Then she
rolled over, revealing an expanse of white shoulder, and settled down to sleep once more.

Carl-Gustav would have these bouts of erotic
insomnia for as long as two or three weeks at a
stretch. He used to lie there on his back, quite still,
eyes wide open, staring at nothing. Then he would
prop himself up on one elbow, slide his hand
under the bedclothes, and caress Freya's warm,
silk-smooth body: her unresponsive breasts, her
hypersensitive belly (another reason why she
hated being touched when she was awake). But on
these occasions she was somewhere else; she had
no knowledge of what was happening to her. Carl-
Gustav's fingers, trembling with repressed desire,

would creep down lower, toward those exquisite, delicate folds of flesh and slide a little way into them. They were warm, dry, devoid of feeling. She would stir in her sleep, and at once he would withdraw his hand and return to his original supine position, cheeks and eyes burning. A fierce desire to cut off the hand that had opened the petals of her inner flesh would surge up in him. One brief moment of contact so sensitized his fingertips that they seemed to acquire an independent existence, somewhere else in space and nothing to do with him, still impregnated with the memory of touching what they had touched. His body was taut with misery and desire and took a long time to subside. Even then the nerves deep under the surface remained in a state of unhealthy irritation.

Normally she slept naked, one more example of her constant mania for nudity. Perhaps—who knows?—she was trying to fend off the suspicion that her body was no more than a kind of garment, with nothing inside it. The garment was *her;* she had no existence beyond its context, its emptiness. She was no more capable of true nakedness than clothes are. But sometimes, in a coquettish mood, she would put on one of her husband's pajama jackets—still keeping up the same natural, forthright pose, the eternal catchphrase: *Well, what's wrong about that?* In the large mirror above the dressing table, facing the bottom of the bed, Carl-Gustav watched both their reflections: two heads, one of them radiantly beautiful, two bodies identically clad in blue silk. Just as if they were lovers or a truly married couple, as if there was some bond between them, as if they had something in common rather than this nothingness.

76

Occasionally, after some hopeless attempt at love making by Carl-Gustav, during which her only reaction had been a series of agonized grimaces, Freya would sprawl back naked across the disordered bedclothes, exposing her hidden charms without a trace of embarrassment—but without the faintest hint of sensuality either. Carl-Gustav was left choking with shame and humiliation and discomfiture. *You have no idea how often I looked at your body—you—and was conscious only of its, your, inaccessibility. Within reach of my hands and body, yet eternally remote. Flesh, yet inanimate matter, a lump, a block.*

Apparently there were other scenes later, distressing and ridiculous incidents that still made his cheeks burn with humiliation when he recalled them for Freya's benefit. One July night he remembered pacing up and down the living room in dressing gown and slippers, holding forth, to use his own words, *with quite idiotic seriousness,* pausing in front of her at intervals and bending down to shout his reproaches in her face. Though it was long after midnight, the air was still mild; through open windows came the laughter of people outside, a glimmer of brightness in the sky. Freya was wearing *your pale blue brocaded silk housecoat, the one that goes so well with your eyes and hair and complexion,* and sat there in an armchair, smoking a cigarette. Carl-Gustav expatiated, in an indignant, rambling manner, on the *intolerable position* she had put him in ever since their tacit agreement (gradually arrived at) to give up physical relations altogether. He went on about his *unsatisfied sexual needs*—not to mention that more subtle sensual passion that left him crazy with desire for something he could never attain and for a personal communion even more impossible.

Freya heard him out, placidly at first and then with some irritation. In her usual sweet way she offered to submit to his advances as best she could. Once or twice she even tried to simulate physical passion herself. But Carl-Gustav was too refined and experienced a sensualist to be taken in by such tricks for a moment; besides, he knew her too well, from way back. The second time it happened he stopped, withdrew from her, and sat there, naked, his head in his hands, jaw muscles quivering with anger, chagrin, and the effort to hold back a flood of tears. Genuinely distressed—though not immoderately so—Freya offered to leave him *if he wanted her to and if she was causing him so much pain.* This statement she delivered in the sort of half-angelic, half-matter-of-fact voice that was just the thing to drive him wild.

I hate you, he wrote, *I shall hate you for the rest of my life. I still hate you even though you have expiated your faults, even though I forgive you. I always forgave you, right from the beginning. Forgiveness and hatred have always coexisted in my heart where you were concerned. The hatred was there at a very early point, not because of any culpable act or intention on your part—you never were guilty of any such thing; far from it, you are totally innocent; you cannot do more, you cannot be other than what you are—but simply due to your existence. I hate you for being, for being this way. For your sensual sterility, for your dried-up heart, for this damned narcissism of yours, this inability to get pleasure from any being except yourself or to give yourself in any way. I hate you be-*

78

*cause I met you and fell in love with you, because I
love you still and cannot help loving you, because
I did not guess the truth soon enough, because I
was not capable of breaking off our relationship
and getting out while there was still time, because
I have used myself up in the idiotic hope that I
might, one day, after a year, maybe—five years,
ten, a lifetime—make you melt and bloom and
ripen under my caresses. I hate you for the same
reason I hate myself—for my ruined life, my
wasted passion, the premature impotence in me
that your own sexlessness brought about.*

I SUSPECT, nonetheless, that he had his own
Achilles' heel somewhere, since any other man
would have sought compensation elsewhere,
would have fallen back on a series of more or less
superficial liaisons that did not involve giving up
Freya. Carl-Gustav, as far as I can make out, never
once felt the least desire for another woman. He
was mesmerized by poor Freya; he kept returning
to the attack in a quite obsessional way—though
at gradually increasing intervals, as his hope of
arousing her diminished. But she was not asleep.
She simply did not exist. He would have had to
create her from scratch.

Little by little his sexual powers became morti-
fied by this involuntary asceticism. Perhaps his
progressive alcoholism had something to do with
it, too. It was Freya's pregnancy that brought their
conjugal relations to an end, however. During this
period she openly admitted to him that the very
idea of sexual intercourse filled her with horror. At

79

Carl-Gustav's first warmly affectionate gesture she would begin to chatter feverishly about the baby. Her maternity was so radiant and touching that Carl-Gustav blushed for his own coarseness in even thinking of her as a mistress.

It is odd that I should have been in possession of so many plain pointers and still failed to understand Freya. I have already admitted my failure to gauge the depth of her frigidity. I should have known this after dancing with her. I only did so once. It was a warm evening, and all the doors and windows were open. Carl-Gustav and Zametti were sitting out on the terrace with drinks and cigars, deep in conversation, watching the moonlight over the water. Michael was playing records. They had an old-fashioned phonograph with a large black and orange striped horn. I can even remember the names of the old-time hit tunes Michael put on: "Let's Dance" and "Sippin' Cider Through a Straw." I can remember the faded silk shade on the standard lamp and the syrupy tone it gave the light. Above all, I remember Michael's expression. There was something sly, unpleasant, and decidedly hostile about it. He remained noticeably silent. Moths fluttered about; their powdery, velvet-soft bodies could be heard bumping against the whitewashed ceiling with a small, clear, tapping sound.

I enjoy dancing, without being particularly good at it. I had already drunk rather too much Nasco, a brew not unlike Tokay, and just as strong, and I was still rather infatuated with Mme. Enquist. To dance with her offered the perfect excuse, at last, for holding her in my arms.

But I have never encountered such a lack of

bodily presence, such clumsiness of movement, and such total deafness to rhythm as Freya displayed that evening. She was eager to dance, said she adored dancing; she pressed herself against me, tossed back her head in order to look me straight in the eye, to dazzle me, to make me dizzy. Then she called out, "Why, Carl-Gustav, he's just as big and strong as you are!"

This was a plain lie. Carl-Gustav was much taller than I was, and at this time especially, when I was still a skinny youth, he could, without effort, have picked me up in one hand, rolled me into a ball, and shoved me out of sight under the nearest piece of furniture. I could feel Freya's flat belly and hard pubis thrust against mine, yet all I felt was her inaccessibility, almost as though she were one of those enchanting cardboard dolls displayed in the windows of fashionable dress shops.

Freya could not get a single step right; she stumbled, trod on my toes, made me tread on hers, got our knees banging against each other; but still she persisted, radiant, adorable, moving in a kind of enchanted dream, convinced, against all the evidence, not only that she was dancing but also that she was dancing *with* someone. It was a heart-breaking sight and, worse, somehow *unreal.* Everybody can dance after a fashion, and everybody knows that really good dancers, men or women, are very rare. Couples who can really dance well together the first time they meet are rarer still, but there is always some degree of co-operation and harmony, however slight, between two bodies following an identical musical rhythm. Freya was not so much lacking in talent as she was the positive embodiment of antitalent, its absence personified. She could not even imagine two rhythms running parallel, let alone counterpointing one another.

Whenever we went out for a trip in the boat, Freya would play at rowing, with Michael, Carl-Gustav, or myself. On such occasions we always put her amidships, with her partner sitting well behind her, where he could keep an eye on her disconnected movements and avoid being clouted by her elbows or sculls. If you had Freya behind you, she was always hammering your spine with her oar grips.

Freya was made to be alone. Yet she was undeniably fascinating: her least glance or smile held a captivating elegance. The moment one came face to face with her, one felt this delectable sense of giddiness and intoxication. I cannot recall anything she said to me, not one word or idea, though we had endless casual conversations over the years —long torrid days on the beach or drinking Vernaccia and Malmsey on the terrace with Carl-Gustav as evening drew on and the sea changed from copper to rose madder and then to a pale silvery blue. Not a word can I recall of all her talk about the natural life, and nudism, and vegetarianism (a chain-smoker, she never drank a drop; perhaps she was scared of cracking the shell of her solitude and succumbing to some nervous depression or hysterical outburst), not to mention theosophy, anthroposophy, Zen Buddhism, occultism, and erotism. Millions of words, and all forgotten now, because there was nothing behind them. I much preferred to watch the movements of her lips as she talked, to look at her face and hair, the invisible halo radiating from her, the quality she had that was *fascinosum,* that mesmerized and glamorized the beholder. As Zametti informed us, with emphatic relish, *fascinum* was the old Latin word for the phallus; *il fallo,* he said, adding that he had some French friends of very ancient and reputable lineage whose family name was Saint-Phalle—"the only saint I could ever bring myself to invoke."

At the same time he hastened to explain that Freya's aura was not so much this crude and shameful priapism as it was Charis, or Grace, the emanation associated with the foam-born goddess, legendary and exquisite creature, white-skinned, violet-eyed, rising from the purple sea—no, not purple, Zametti said, his improbable French accent well to the fore, rather the color of wine lees: *epi oinopa ponton,* as Homer put it, "over the wine-dark sea."

IT FOLLOWS that Carl-Gustav was lying, more or less deliberately, when he asserted that his reasons for abandoning a university career and retiring into the wilderness were purely intellectual. This declaration took place during a conversation he had with Zametti and myself one summer night out on the terrace. It was not the occasion on which I made my abortive attempt to dance with Freya, but some time afterward. She was not there that evening; she and Michael had gone out for a trip in the boat.

There was only a single lamp lit; it stood on the table amid a litter of bottles and glasses and cigars. Our wickerwork basket chairs were full of holes no one had bothered to mend, and every change of position produced creaks and groans from the worn rattan. The night air was vibrant with the high-pitched chirping of cicadas, and this sound seemed to reecho from the dark, velvet-smooth clouds hanging over the mountains. Not a leaf stirred; the sea lay smooth as a mirror. The air was still and electric. We had expected a storm, but after tossing and turning all through the night, sweating, scarcely able to breathe, bedclothes scattered on the floor, I had awakened to another equally baking day. The clouds had moved on inland. You could almost feel the thin topsoil on the hills crumble into fine dust as those stifling shadows passed slowly over them. Every now and then we caught a pleasant scent in the air, aromatic exhalations of fast-ebbing sap from the *maquis*.

The dinner, cooked by Assunta and served by Giusta, had been far too heavy. Sufarri and favata, especially the latter, are dishes that should be kept for cold weather. But Freya could not be bothered with housekeeping and ate very little herself, hurrying through meals with little concern for proper nourishment. As a result we were forced to plow through what these peasant women considered dinners fit for *signori*. The stupefying effect of this regimen was still further increased by the Nasco, which left our brains dull and sluggish. Only Zametti still had his wits about him that evening; but then he had carefully restricted himself to two glasses of wine throughout. Carl-Gustav and I were both fairly torpid, though there was something both tense and irritating about the atmosphere that kept us from relaxing completely.

The professor was determined to force some kind of confession out of his host. "I can't understand you at all," he was saying. "It's still a complete mystery to me. With an intellect like yours, and such natural talent, and that brilliant early academic career—"

"I've lost all interest in that sort of thing," Carl-Gustav said. His voice was quite amiable; although he acutely disliked talking about himself, he managed to conceal the fact very well on this occasion. He looked Zametti straight in the eye and added, with a smile, "I came to see my true insignificance."

Zametti raised his neat plump hands in protest, but Carl-Gustav went on, his voice as courteous as ever, "It's quite true, I assure you. That is why I chose this insignificant village and way of life, among insignificant people—"

"But what about scholarship? Archaeology—"

"Archaeology, my dear professor," said Carl-Gustav, laughing, "is of great practical value as a description of the future." And he began to talk about the sites of various ancient civilizations, such as those in the Near East and north China, pointing out how barren and deserted they seemed now. He slipped into a scientific parody of Zametti's digressive mannerisms, partly to amuse him, partly as an exercise in his most characteristic vein of bland and inscrutable mockery. "Nothing to see but insignificant tumuli, acres of debris littered with potsherds and old stones, visited only by a few starving nomads. What will be left of our great modern cities? Even less. Paper soon crumbles, rust devours steel. The only indestructible objects will be those celluloid films that escape the holocaust and anything made from plastic—toothbrushes, buckets, containers for detergents and deodorants . . ."

He amused himself by sounding off against the peasants, who, according to him, regarded all ancient monuments as convenient open-cast quarries, and in particular against all goatherds, "those enemies of civilization—wherever the goat has passed through, nothing remains in the end but barren steppes. Temples and palaces, universities and stock markets, all collapse into identical anonymous mounds of rubble, and on every one of them you'll find goats, munching up everything in sight."

He paused. "That's why I like the people here. They show me the final scene in the drama. Here I can detest humanity—and know precisely why I do so. Oh, what a boring, futile, endlessly repetitive comedy—will you have another drink? Personally, I find this hot, dry atmosphere makes me very thirsty. It's extraordinary the way the rain's still holding off this year."

He began to pour out wine for us; the professor made a gentle yet somehow unctuous gesture of refusal.

"Come to think of it," Carl-Gustav added, "it does the same thing every year." He was a seething mass of impotence, desire, and frustration, yet despite this he now launched into a mild attack on archaeologists, who, he said, had ruined archaeology for him.

Zametti turned to me in distress and said, "The real culprits are these ghastly Sardinian peasants, *questi disgraziati*—*they're* the ones who've made him what he is today. He's living among savages. Did you read what happened to those unfortunate English tourists? It was all in the papers."

86

I had indeed seen the report, in *The Times*, before leaving Rome. A middle-aged couple on a walking trip through the Barbagia area—or it may have been Gallura, I can't remember—had been found by some shepherds, lying beside their picnic things, shot dead. Nothing had been taken. The Thermos bottles were untouched; a pile of sandwiches still sat there on an open paper napkin.

"I really must defend these Sardinian neighbors of mine," Carl-Gustav said, reaching out for the Nasco. "They are men of honor. And the last thing they want is any trouble likely to harm the tourist trade. Two days after that little incident, the murderer was recognized in a bar and shot, at point-blank range. No one could identify these, ah, dispensers of justice. Or so they said. Another drink?"

"Thanks," I said, "I'd love one." I could feel my head growing heavy. Carl-Gustav's speech was beginning to slur. We were interrupted by the sudden appearance of Lupu, who materialized, abruptly and noiselessly, out of the velvet darkness and stood there, three paces from us, holding himself very straight.

"What do you want?" Carl-Gustav asked him.

"It's about the men's work tomorrow morning. What shall I tell them to do?" Lupu's voice was neutral.

Carl-Gustav excused himself and exchanged a few words privately with his foreman. I imagine it concerned some job that had to be done in the vineyard, which was slowly, year by year, going to ruin. When he came back he looked very much put out. Lupu had disappeared.

Zametti said, "That boor is the very worst kind

of Sardinian. What an unpleasant lout! *Che mascalzone!* Why the devil do you keep him on?"

When he replied, Carl-Gustav's jauntily casual manner suggested a man who owns a dangerous dog he is very fond of and has no intention of destroying, despite the remonstrances of bitten, or merely frightened, neighbors.

"You know, I find him a very accomplished fellow—very accomplished indeed in his own way. These peasants may be destitute, but they've still got their pride. Not one of them would ever take a job in service. They want to be free. They always have been, too. None of your landed gentry in Sardinia, despite the Spanish occupation. Lupu doesn't regard himself as a servant. He's doing me a favor. I'm the one who's obliged to him. Besides, it's no more than the truth. I depend on him more than he depends on me. I need him. By the way, he's one of your political comrades, professor, did you realize? I don't know whether he still carries a Party card, but he's always ready in an emergency."

AT THIS POINT Carl-Gustav gave us a cheerful account of how the *carabinieri* came back at the end of the war, after the American troops had pulled out. One autumn afternoon he happened to be standing on this same terrace, his hands in his pockets, surveying the scene before him—the gun-metal sea, streaked with yellow and gray, the black islands, the deserted road winding its way across the promontory, while great waves, inaudible at this distance, exploded on the shore below.

Above this desolate expanse the sky was gray and cloudy, except for the occasional rift of cold bright light. The village below nestled snugly between two shoulders of hill, half-hidden in its wooded hollow, with only two or three rooftops and the church spire showing through. You could just see the corner of the street leading to the Maddalena, a flat, fragmented space without so much as a dog stirring on it. A puddle gleamed in the sunlight. Then a canvas-topped military truck appeared and vanished into the distance again. That was all. Carl-Gustav gave it not a moment's thought; he was absolutely indifferent to whatever might be happening down below.

About an hour later—dusk had not yet begun to fall, and the light was still more or less the same—there came the sound of dogs barking and men's voices. Carl-Gustav, who was in his work room and sitting idly at his work table—for some time he had done no work whatsoever—went out to see what was going on. Down beyond the house, on the old sunken track leading up to it, he saw a group of soldiers. They were hurrying along, cursing and grumbling, beneath the big retaining wall and its withered, yellowing vinecreepers, bareheaded, collars unbuttoned, some even with tunics gaping open to reveal the shirt underneath. They looked not only untidy but singularly unmilitary. Yet they were assuredly not civilians either. They looked like one thing, and one only: beaten troops, retreating in disorder. Some of them appeared to have lost their belts. Others wore them unbuckled, swinging loose on their thighs as they walked. They had no weapons at all, not one rifle or bayonet between them. Their faces were red, their hair either ruffled into spikes or glued to their temples with sweat. They seemed a very pig-headed lot indeed, and although they were muttering among themselves, they were not exactly forthcoming to anyone else. They barely acknowledged Carl-Gustav's questions, tramped across the courtyard without even stopping, and went on their way, a loose-strung, disorderly file that dwindled slowly among the vineyards and the *maquis*-covered outcrops, following the track that led to the nuraghe. Soon the light began to fade, and it was only just possible to make them out, dotted along the slanting path on the hillside. Finally they vanished altogether.

They were, in fact, the local police force. When the village became a front-line area they had been evacuated, but now they had come back to take over their duties once more. These returning *carabinieri* found their station in an appalling mess. The walls were filthy, any windows still unbroken were thick with grime, doors had been removed bodily, the floor was a litter of rubble and ceiling-plaster, and heaps of excrement had accumulated in every corner.

Ten minutes after the departure of the truck that had brought them to the village, their post was surrounded by a dozen peasants armed with shotguns. All down the street shutters were hastily closed. Two or three children went scampering home as fast as they could, in response to shrill and peremptory summonses from their invisible mothers.

The peasants were all wearing red armbands. Training their shotguns on the *carabinieri*, they made them hand over rifles, pistols, hand grenades, the sergeant's revolver, and the station Bren gun.

After this they told them to get out. They stood and watched while their victims sloped off, slouching along in hang-dog fashion, shoulders slumped, feet dragging. A barely visible sardonic grin flickered across one or two faces, but for the most part the spectators looked as they always did; morose, down-to-earth, and grimly serious.

"Lupu was one of them," Carl-Gustav told us, with a wry laugh. "Now they've all got guns hidden away somewhere—buried probably, heavily oiled and wrapped in rags. I wouldn't be surprised if they lined the hole with slabs of cork, too, just as their ancestors used to."

This was a reference to special hollow niches, let into the Cyclopean masonry of certain nuraghes, in particular the giant Losa nuraghe, which stands on the lonely upland plateau of Abbasanta, in the heart of the shepherd's domain. Remains of cork slabs were found adhering to the sides of these arms caches. The cork oak still grows in Sardinia. You often see specimens as you cross the countryside, their trunks stripped bare, circumcised, bleeding, suggestive of a crude and menacing obscenity connected not so much with sensuous pleasure as with notions of wounding, agony, castration.

CARL-GUSTAV and Lupu would often chat together during the evening, Carl-Gustav sitting at his work table, the neolithic mortar in front of him overflowing with cigarette butts, while Lupu remained standing. He never sat down in his employer's house, and Carl-Gustav never invited him to do so. Lupu would either lean against the wall or against the frame of the open doorway, as though he wanted to keep a line of retreat open behind him.

"He's got a very special brand of caution and wariness, just like a wild animal," Carl-Gustav used to say. His tone of amused admiration contained a hint of unconscious contempt. "I don't mean the way he moves—there he's quite human; he looks just like the peasant he is. No, it's this trick he's got of always being on the alert, of being ready to face any possible contingency. He's got his defenses deployed the whole time—there's always a couple of bolt holes laid on for him if he needs them. No one's ever going to take *him* by surprise or catch him off guard."

Lupu, for his part, both respected and despised Carl-Gustav, though for very different reasons. To begin with, the Swede was twice his size and twice as strong in the bargain—although Lupu himself had tremendous stamina. "In his company," Carl-Gustav said, "he was always the man who got stuck with the job of carrying the machine gun. Think of it, thirty-mile treks over the mountains with all that hardware on your back!" On the other hand, from Lupu's point of view his employer was a scholar, someone who read books; and this was a demeaning activity for any man, only perhaps to be condoned in a priest. Besides, there was that other business . . .

"*HOW DID* you kill the fascists?" Carl-Gustav asked. "Tell me the story." It had been an empty, boring day; now he was sitting in the dark, long after everyone else was asleep. Most of the time he had no guests in the house; nothing happened and there was very little conversation, since none of them had anything to say to each other.

Lupu was lounging half in and half out of the open door. The left side of his body formed a silhouette against the starry sky; the right was lost in shadow.

"How?" he muttered. "What d'you mean, *how?* The usual way."

"At night?"

"Yes. At night."

"Come on, tell me."

"They were brought out of the mayor's office. That's where they'd been locked up all day. Had to get rid of their wives first. There wasn't anyone around on the square then. It was late, too. Drove them out of the village to a spot by the cemetery. Brought spades and shovels along. Come on, they were told, get digging. So they dug their own graves. Deeper, we told them, deeper—don't want the dogs to dig you up, do you? One young kid was crying. The mayor's son. He was fifteen."

Lupu turned and spat over his shoulder, out onto the terrace.

"Did—did they all die the same way? Even the youngsters?" Carl-Gustav was filled with what he afterward described as a *feeling of shameful but irresistible curiosity, like the time I could not stop myself asking you much too detailed and personal questions about your physical relationship with Eklundh.*

"Of course. All the males, in every family. Finish the thing off, get done with it. Otherwise we'd have had endless blood feuds on our hands."

"Yes. I suppose you would. Tell me one more thing. Was it done facing them or in the back?"

"In the back. Straight through the heart. Then the graves were filled in. But next day their wives dug them up again and took them into the church and from there to the cemetery. What must be must be, right?"

"You're not a religious man, are you?" Carl-Gustav asked.

"No. What *we* need are schools and technical training and tractors, not processions, that's why. But the women have got to have all the trimmings —they need 'em. Men, too," Lupu added, and Carl-Gustav sensed, rather than saw, the sneer on his face. Then there was the sound of a match being struck, and in the flame Lupu's features sprang out clear: square-cut swarthy face, straight eyebrows, stone-hard eyes, fine, deep-scored lines and wrinkles. He flicked the match onto the terrace, and all that remained was the red glow of his cigarette.

"All priests are stupid bastards," Lupu growled. "But they're nothing compared to the *marescialli*. A policeman's the biggest, stupidest bastard on God's earth, as cowardly as he is miserable. These *carabinieri* torture anyone they arrest, just as Jesus Christ was tortured." He paused. "Of course, Christ was a communist." Carl-Gustav knew he was shaking with silent laughter, though his face remained hidden in shadow.

"But they're scared, you know. Especially since that fellow from Orgosolo knocked off six of them at one go, over in Sa Verula. What's more, he's killed Niccolo, Giovanni, and Antonio Taras too, three of the nastiest stool pigeons in these parts.

94

Oh, he's got a price on his head now, five million lire, no less. And he still comes and goes as he likes in the Nuoro country, free as air."

Carl-Gustav said, "The *carabinieri* aren't exactly popular down in the village, are they, Lupu?"

"If they mind their own business and leave us in peace," Lupu said with contemptuous indifference, "nothing will happen to them. This *maresciallo* we've got now, Atzeni, isn't too bad. He knows damn well that one fine day the balloon's going up around here, and when it does, what chance has *he* got of finding anywhere to hide? So Atzeni watches his step. Nothing happens in this district. No stool pigeons either. There isn't time to sit and think about this or that. It's a tough life. Work your guts out."

Having reached the portentous platitude stage, they both fell silent but continued to smoke peacefully in the darkness, one sitting, the other still on his feet, facing his master.

IN THE BACK. Straight through the heart. Carl-Gustav himself would never have lifted a finger against anybody. He was the very embodiment of gentle amiability. His first overriding emotion was astonishment that he felt no trace of repugnance at the idea of Lupu, whom he saw daily, being a murderer. For Carl-Gustav, there were no fine shades to homicide. A killer was always a killer; or rather, a murder was always an assassination. His cut-and-dried attitude was conditioned by the fact that he wholeheartedly opposed the death penalty and was an equally determined supporter of psychotherapeutical treatment for criminals, whom he regarded as either seriously ill people or the victims of social pressures. The very idea of bloodshed turned him cold.

Yet he by no means disliked Lupu. Indeed, he found much to admire in him: his rough vigor and energy, his animal cunning. But he despised him too, with that scornful pity he reserved for children and animals. Since he knew very well that Lupu was not mentally unstable, he ascribed the massacre of the fascists to his cruelly barbarous environment. Indeed, he regarded all peasants as belonging to a quite different species and would never have dreamed of treating them as equals. Such a notion he found utterly ridiculous. For him they were adult children.

Both he and Freya were always delighted when the two couples, together with old Assunta, decked themselves out in their national costume on the feast day of the local patron saint, Saint Lusorio. For once Lupu and Pascal would get out of their working clothes—military denims kept after demobilization—and change into black sheepskin boleros, wide-sleeved white shirts, baggy cloth breeches ballooning out over their thighs, gaiters, and the characteristic Sardinian beret. This last each of them wore in his own fashion. Pascal's drooped down at the back between his shoulders, which made him look like the booby he was; Lupu's tilted jauntily over one temple. Both of them behaved with a stiff ceremonial formality. The Enquists were touched by this naïve exhibitionism and found it quite delightfully amusing.

Freya, like Carl-Gustav, had never regarded Lupu as a man. By way of returning the compliment, Lupu did not look on her as a woman. She would go around almost naked in his presence, her beautiful breasts half-exposed, and when she spoke to him she would—quite unconsciously and without forethought—thrust this luscious décolleté under his nose.

Lupu would answer her in a stiff, respectful manner, always fixing his eyes firmly on her face; not once, in the course of these ten or fifteen years, had he so much as glanced at her bare shoulders. It was as though she were wearing a suit of armor. For him she was not a woman; she was his employer's wife. He was a Sardinian, and in his local patois they used the word *stimaï*, from *estimare*, for "to love deeply and passionately," *amaï* for the love one bore toward God, and *cozzare*, which literally means "to poke," for the sexual act, between humans or animals. There was no place for the *professore's signora* in these clearly drawn categories. He used to talk freely and seriously with her, just as he might with Carl-Gustav, and not by the faintest nuance did he ever acknowledge the difference between them.

He was the only man you never tried to arouse, Carl-Gustav wrote. *Were you afraid of him, I wonder? He stank of cattle and wool grease. He had that great mat of hair showing through the dirty old shirt he wore ; it made him look as if he had on a black sheepskin undershirt. Did all this scare you?* But in fact she was not even remotely frightened of Lupu. She feared nothing and nobody.

Perhaps I do Lupu too much honor. "They're not human beings," Professor Zametti used to say, with a chuckle, "they're *Sardinians*." I would prefer, myself, to reverse his meaning, making it rather more complimentary to the islanders. Perhaps Lupu was not a Sardinian first and foremost but a man like other men; perhaps he *did* want Freya. If so, nobody knew it, least of all the Enquists themselves. But then they would never have noticed in any case, would never have so much as considered the possibility. Yet there was just one pointer, albeit an indirect one, and that was Freya's instant antipathy toward him, right from the start.

"He's insolent," she would tell Carl-Gustav. "You've got to get rid of him."

"Has he been disrespectful to you in any way?"

"No. It's just the ways he looks at me—"

"How *does* he look at you?"

"As though I were an animal, a cow or something—"

"But in that case," Carl-Gustav said, laughing, "I presume lust doesn't come into it? You don't suspect him of bestiality, do you?"

"Oh, you don't *understand!*" she cried. But despite her irritation, Carl-Gustav refused to budge and Lupu stayed on.

I know exactly what you had against him, darling. He was my opposite. For me you were a goddess; for him you were nothing. I had become impotent through love for you, whereas he would have possessed you, anywhere, at any time, in any circumstances, with utter indifference. I had to have this man near me. I kept him as a kind of antidote against you . . . Without even knowing how, I sensed that one day he would serve as the instrument to effect my cure.

One summer night Freya, giggling, said to Carl-

Gustav, "Can you imagine Lupu and that hunch-backed wife of his making love?"

He shrugged. "It's none of my business." She caused him almost unbearable irritation by bringing up such topics and did so all too frequently. That particular night Lupu and the rest were sleeping out of doors, somewhere in the hayfield behind the house. The sky overhead was bright with tremulous stars, and from every quarter came the deafening racket of cicadas in full cry. The twinkling of the constellations might have been the visible effect produced by this shrill interminable sound ascending from the parched earth below.

On another very similar night Carl-Gustav was strolling barefoot through the fields—though it was past twelve, the air remained baking hot—when he heard people talking nearby: Lupu and Ignazia, bedded down in the straw behind a haycock. They were discussing him and Freya.

"She has *su demònio*," Ignazia said, in her dryly passionate voice. "And he does nothing to stop her. Hasn't the man got eyes in his head?"

The male voice articulated one clear word in response: *Corrudu*.

Corrudu, my sweet, Carl-Gustav wrote, *is the Sardinian version of cornuto, cornutus, the cuckold, the horned one. In this case, me. These wretched creatures have been despising me from the bottom of their hearts, night and day, for years. Oh, you don't deceive me, I know that, though it's only because the impulse happens to be lacking in you. And yet they're right, all the same. Here am I, wronged, deceived, robbed of my manhood. You may enjoy playing Beauty, but I have no relish for*

99

the role of the Beast—and that is what I have be-
come, thanks to you. Don't worry, I'm not blaming
you. I am the one who must bear the responsibility
—for my feebleness and inertia, for failing to
shake off the yoke while there was still time, for
not bucking when I first felt its weight on my neck.
The onetime bull is now the mildest, most patient
of oxen. Poor creature.

SO ALL the time he was holding forth in so
learned and amiable a fashion, with his witty
parody of Zametti's wilder speculations, his mind
was a hotbed of slowly fermenting rage and humiliation—that archaic humiliation from which no
one, however civilized, is ultimately immune.

"And above all, *caro professore*," he was saying,
"don't talk to me about 'Mediterranean clarity';
the phrase has no meaning unless you're making a
weather report. You might instead take a good
look at Homer, with his gorily professional descrip-
tions of warriors' wounds—not to mention his
priest-kings, who first kill the sacrificial ox, then
dismember it, and 'wrap fat skillfully about the
victims' thighs.' It's all too much like an open-air
restaurant, customers and all. The Olympian reli-
gion stinks of barbecued meat, and all those
solemn prayers on the Acropolis were addressed
to a turnspit goddess, armed to the teeth like a
paratrooper!"

He was interrupted by the arrival of Freya and
Michael. They swam into our vision side by side,
at the far end of the terrace, so tall and bright that
it was as if they possessed some inner source of

radiance. The effect was probably due to nothing more mysterious than their summer clothes, their fair hair, and a certain pallor induced by long hours of rowing and swimming, together with the hard climb up from the shore. But seeing them again in my mind's eye, I still cannot help but regard their sudden appearance as something akin to a nocturnal blossoming. Their fresh bright beauty had no more in common with this parched, intense, mysterious darkness than do certain night-blooming flowers—scented and colorless, innocently fleshy calyx open wide—have with the dark, rough foliage from which they spring.

I cannot remember, after all this time, whether Zametti went into one of his rapturous Isis-and-Osiris ecstasies, but he would certainly have had some justification for doing so. Freya was wearing a light cotton dress and I suspect, not another stitch underneath it; Michael had on a T-shirt and an old pair of white jeans, bleached by constant scrubbing. Both of them were barefoot. Under those golden halos their faces seemed like masks—smooth, relaxed, softened by swimming into a more-than-natural beauty. On the other hand, I have no illusions about how the effect was created. The only light came from a single hurricane lamp on the garden table—I remember the burned insects scattered all around it—that gave the kind of feeble light calculated to enhance their appearance in a way that left us breathless with admiration.

"We've been swimming in the sea," Freya said, radiant as ever. "The water was so lovely and smooth and warm—just like fresh milk."

I winced. The remark was absolutely typical,

right in Freya's most phony and artificial vein. But perhaps it wasn't this slight offense against good taste that really annoyed me. I had, I suppose, a touch of impotent jealousy. I too had been on those private boat excursions, sometimes with all three of them, sometimes just myself, Freya, and Michael. I knew that exquisite, half-hypnotized feeling one got from the warm air and scarcely less warm water; I remembered the smell of mint and myrtle, wafted seaward on each random breeze from the scrub-laden hills; I could hear the gentle chuckle of ripples against the moving boat, the drowsy rhythm of the sculls, the faint creak of the oarlocks.

I still had a vision of Michael sitting in the bow while I held the tiller, his arm muscles bunching with concentrated effort, lazily powerful tendons sliding under the honey-marble skin of his torso. He had large, fleshy shoulders and a very slim waist. He would bend forward, then fling himself back, his eyes half-closed. We were gliding along in the shadow of the promontory, toward the luminous indigo expanse, darkness all stippled with silver, that opened beyond the last rock of the headland, an enchanting vista through which one could gladly have voyaged on forever, lost to the world. An intensely sensuous yet elusive feeling, like the quiet breathing of a garden at night, slowly stole over me, soothing my body and my nerves, filling them with an erotic awareness as deep as it was ill-defined.

I turned away from Freya and Michael and walked across to the balustrade of the terrace, hands in pockets, a cigar in my mouth, pretending to be absorbed by that infinite mirrored expanse

Zametti called the "multiple laughter of the sea," *to toû pontou gélasma,* asleep now under the moon.

But I could sense their presence behind me and strained my ears to catch anything that was said. My nerves had been tried by a number of things that night: the dry, electric air, an overheavy dinner, too much strong wine, too many cigarettes, and now an upsurge of jealousy provoked by this nocturnal apparition. I have a very clear recollection of Carl-Gustav's suddenly chilly and ironic tone of voice as he inquired—with a superficial show of politeness—what sort of trip they had had. The gravity of the situation never struck me at the time, and Freya and Michael were equally oblivious. Indeed, they continued to underestimate it for some while to come. I at least observed this new, barely definable change of atmosphere; but I never paused to consider its implications.

THIS WAS a year or two after Michael had gone away to boarding school. He was already a man physically and as sturdy as his father. He would row effortlessly for hours—the slave once more—never saying a word, a bleached lock of hair falling over his forehead, blue eyes staring grimly from beneath that heavy ridged brow. His expression no longer struck me as devious, but seemed rather concentrated, distracted. When Michael smiled— a rare occurrence—his normally tight-shut mouth became soft and full, like a child's. Women were going to find him irresistible. Freya fell in love with him the first time he came back from school for the holidays.

Probably she always had been, right from the first, though far too lacking in self-awareness or detachment to know it consciously. Carl-Gustav, on the other hand, had sensed the truth during the first months of Michael's life, when Freya blocked his tentative advances, the last he ever made, by talking about the baby. So Carl-Gustav became a devoted father. Much later, however, he found a way to get back at Freya while looking after his son's best interests.

"We've got to send the boy to school," he said. "Honestly, darling, I can't go on hiring a succession of tutors forever. He'll turn into a little savage if he stays here. It's downright unhealthy for him. I don't want to jeopardize his future."

And all the time I was talking, he wrote, *I had one eye on your reactions. I was waiting for the first shock as the idea went home. I was looking forward with some enjoyment to your frantic, flimsy arguments in favor of keeping him at home with you. I wanted to relish your agony of mind, unconscious perhaps, unadmitted, and indeed inadmissible, since my attitude was so reasonable, so convincing. You have given me few pleasures in recent years, but this was certainly one of them. The other main one, of course, was seeing you naked, and here the pleasure came mingled with so much pain. I have for long relished the cunning way in which I eliminated first Paris ("His companions would take him straight off to a whorehouse—if not worse"), and then Rome ("where at least he would have less opportunity for contracting curious liaisons"), remarks that—as I did not fail to observe—left you tense and frozen with anxiety. The joke is, of course, that I made them in all seriousness. I meant every word I said; I would have taken the same line whatever the circumstances to safeguard Michael's own best interests when discussing the problems with his mother—a real mother, who had no objection to being called Mama. Yet my words took on very special significance and flavor when addressed to their pseudo-lover who had taught the boy to call her by a false name, whose relationship to him was no longer that of a mother only and who had altogether ceased to be his father's wife.*

MICHAEL had been really taken aback by the noisy outburst of sobs and weeping that greeted his departure. He had no idea what lay behind Freya's behavior and found it a great embarrassment to have her hanging around his neck and spraying tears all over his face. *After all,* he wrote, *I wasn't going off to the wars or on a polar expedition or something. She really had no reason to carry on in such a way—especially when I myself was so excited at the prospect of seeing new places and meeting so many new people.* But he was touched by her distress nevertheless. "Poor darling Freya," he told himself. "All mothers are like that, I suppose." He comforted her as best he could—*though somewhat perfunctorily, I fear, since my mind was already on the journey ahead of me.*

He may not have known why you were crying, Marie, Carl-Gustav wrote, *but you did. You knew all right. You felt instinctively that it was over, that you had lost him. When he came back here for the holidays, growing taller and handsomer every time, more and more a person in his own right, and thus more detached from you, increasingly alien, you lost your head. At last it was your turn, my love. The object of your passion always escaped you, remained elusive and inaccessible, forever beyond your grasp and imbued with just the same cruel compassion that you bestowed on me. You were luckier than I was, though; he has always loved you more than you loved me; he has always regretted the suffering he caused you more than you ever dreamed of regretting the harm you did to me. You had more luck than I did—but it was still not enough.*

One thing among the many he could never forgive Freya was the ridiculous night she inflicted on him when Michael ran away from home. Beside herself with fury, she demanded—insisted—that her husband go after the fugitive and bring him back. Carl-Gustav had an old Ford locked up in a lean-to behind the Maddalena, always tanked up and ready, but sometimes left six months between trips. He got it out, drove down to Sassari, and went around every brothel in town—to the jeers of the prostitutes and their clients—till finally he found Michael, pale, defiant, and very much ashamed of himself, and hauled him off home.

It was very late when they got in, and all the lights in the house had been turned off. But as they felt their way through the dark, a cold and cutting voice came from the open door of Freya's room, slashing into them like a razor. "Filthy beast," it hissed. "Dirty little guttersnipe. Couldn't you control yourself any longer? Disgusting pig! Well, do you feel better now, you repulsive object?

Losing your virginity to some common whore, some crabbed-up *scaïa*—"

She burst into tears. *I had no idea,* Carl-Gustav wrote, venomously, *that you possessed so wide and subtle a range of expressions.* But at the time he obediently did what she told him; he was inured to her whims by now, broken in, submissive. On top of everything else he was dead tired, sickened by what he had done, and desperately sorry for Michael. The worst of it all, in a way, was that it had been a complete failure. Michael had still not found the courage to do anything by the time his father discovered him.

You really tortured him, didn't you? Carl-Gustav wrote. *For years on end you kept him bursting with frustration—unless he found out the other wretched alternative. You did him the greatest possible harm, greater even than the pair of you afterward did to me. Were those moonlight excursions fun? What did you talk about during them? I used to ask myself. Now I know. You didn't exchange a word of real conversation. There you were, perfectly happy, reeling off a lot of vacuous chatter, while he kept rowing, so patient and taciturn, and had fantasies about his Swiss girl friends. What a joke the whole thing was! And there was I, feeling snubbed and shut out of what I took to be your private paradise!*

HIS ALCOHOLISM and increasingly neurotic state of mind led Carl-Gustav to develop a morbid fixation on Michael. He watched the boy grow steadily taller and more dazzlingly good-looking, while at the same time he felt himself aging, becoming more decrepit. He slept badly and for shorter periods. His brain was muzzy, his mind inert and sterile, his masculinity reduced. *Michael never knew it,* Carl-Gustav wrote, *but his very existence was a standing humiliation to me. He could go on rowing for hours after I was out of breath and energy. He would still be swimming effortlessly half an hour after I had been forced back to shore for fear of drowning. Watching him through adolescence, seeing him grow into manhood—and obviously shaping up to be twice the man I was at his age—meant, also, observing my own progressive decrepitude. For the first time I became aware emotionally rather than intellectually, that I was going to die. I found it only too easy to picture his reaction when I did—bearing the loss of his father with manly fortitude, comforting his mother, and, as a good son should, taking over the duties, on her behalf, of this contemptible and now defunct husband.*

Quarrels began to flare up between Michael and his father. It was always Carl-Gustav who began them, but worse than the quarrels were some of the man-to-man discussions they had, as though between two close friends, during which Michael would, quite unintentionally, wound Carl-Gustav's feelings simply because he was a man, not a child, and thus no longer an extension of his father's personality. Carl-Gustav described one of these occasions to Freya, with an obsessional wealth of detail. They were sitting out in front of the house, legs crossed, smoking, two men enjoying each other's company. Michael said, with that casual air of superiority so characteristic of a young student, "I can see why you gave up archaeology. In the last resort it's limited to the establishment of facts. Not even that, really—just a provisional framework of guesses and inferences and theories, all very uncertain and liable to be upset by the next excavation. No basis for establishing any coherent general pattern. Whereas in any discipline amenable to mathematical laws, I can make valid predictions. I have a firm base to stand on. Any theorem developed in accordance with the system of axioms I accept—provided they do not contain some contradiction—will be as true today as it was in the time of the nuraghe builders. Have you ever considered the possibility of applying the theory of games to—"

He broke off, remembering, too late, that his father was not a mathematician. This show of tact, and the condescension it implied, merely intensified Carl-Gustav's sense of humiliation. Michael too was slipping away from him—but by overtaking him, outstripping him man to man, on equal terms.

"Of course, it's all a matter of symbols," Michael went on hastily, doing his best in the face of Carl-Gustav's silent, freezing smile. "You just have to select the appropriate language and a metalanguage that enables you to set up terms of critical reference—"

Carl-Gustav interrupted him at this point. He spoke to Michael as one might speak to a stranger, a stranger, moreover, that was despised and to whom one would not hesitate to be grossly impolite.

"I find everything you've been telling me very edifying and instructive, dear boy, but too boring

for words. I just can't take any more of it." And
with that he got up and walked away, trembling
with fury.

THERE WERE months of tension, interspersed
with periods of calm and affection. But suddenly
Carl-Gustav would revert to his surly, taciturn,
sneering mood. *I couldn't repeat one malicious or
unkind remark you made,* Michael wrote, *but
that's because I deliberately tried to forget them. I
suppressed every word. I have no recollection of
anything you said.* But there was one exception.
It was early morning, I gather, and Michael was
out in the courtyard, sitting under the walnut tree,
gazing at the ivy and Virginia creeper that clus-
tered over the buttress wall against the hillside.
It was a beautiful day—everything very green,
blue sky, clear pure light. Then Carl-Gustav
walked by, *stooping a little, pipe clenched between
your teeth. You made some nasty little crack as you
passed me—"Great brain at work, I see," or "Lazy-
bones"; something of that sort—but it isn't what
you actually said that's important. What I can still
see is your sickly, sneering grin—and to think I
idolized you throughout my childhood! You hated
me—and I had no idea why. What could I do to
win back your friendship? What had I done to lose
it?*

HE UNDERSTOOD in the end, though at first he
dared not believe the truth. *I had gone away. I had
left you, yet I never stopped belonging to you and*

with you, I never faltered in my love for you. But the first time he came back home on vacation he knew he had become detached from them. All at once everything looked different. The mountains were mere hills, the village houses slum hovels; their inhabitants looked little better than beggars, and the Maddalena, as he said, *looked as though she was suffering from some sort of liver complaint.* Under that blazing sun even the sea looked commonplace, and the beach was a narrow, dirty strip of sand, littered with wreckage. *I cannot forgive myself for finding you smaller, less good-looking, and, above all, older than I remembered you.*

Later, after he had been back a number of times and had met and gotten to know various new friends, *I finally came to see what odd people you were*—he had written *special* to begin with, then carefully crossed the word out, in such a way that I could barely decipher it—*and how utterly different Freya is from my friends' mothers. Since she had brought me up to regard it as something quite natural, I was never surprised when I saw her naked—indeed, I never really looked at her. Not once! Certainly not in that particular way, with that particular kind of curiosity, that direct and deliberate stare. I don't like to think of it even now. I was never bothered about being naked myself when she was around either. But I did begin to feel a bit embarrassed when she kept up that little game of helping me wash myself. I was afraid I might offend her if I admitted how I felt. She'd have replied, "Well, there's nothing wrong about that, is there? After all, I'm your mother." So I let her go on pouring water over me and scrubbing my back.*

There was no bathroom in the Enquists' house, just a stone-paved recess, to which Assunta and Giusta brought relays of large beaten-copper pans filled with hot water. Family and guests alike bathed in the same manner, by standing there and sluicing themselves down.

Once when she was examining me she began to stare at, well, one particular part with absolute fascination. "You're so big and strong," she said. "You'll have to be careful with women—you might easily hurt them." "For heaven's sake," I said. I felt horribly embarrassed and half-turned away to hide myself. I still maintain she wasn't thinking of herself in this context. She really meant no harm. She just had no idea what was happening to her. All her life she had believed (and had succeeded in convincing me) that nakedness, ours in particular, was pure and innocent, that physical love-making was wholly unimportant. One day—I cannot remember where or when, or in what connection; all that remains with me is her anxious expression and the lie I told her—she said to me, "You're not going to let that have any importance in your life, are you? Mere momentary pleasure. You won't, will you? Tell me you won't—" I have forgotten my exact response, but I am quite sure, recalling my own ignorance and submissiveness, that it must have been "Of course not." Yet I remember being quite sure that the opposite was true; I knew perfectly well I didn't believe what I was saying. I just wanted to please her. Anyway, as far as I was concerned she stood right outside this side of my life and personality, always had done, always would do. I mean what I say when I tell you, again, that for me she was sacred, untouchable.

He went on to explain how, during their trips in the boat, they would sometimes get out on the underwater sandbank that formed an extension of the promontory. You have to know the exact spot, because everywhere else is deep water; but you can stand on the sandbank—the sea only comes up to your waist. They used to strip off and swim around the boat naked, and then she would tell him to soap her back. He would do so, his eyes fixed on the horizon, watching the advancing shadows as twilight drew on. *But I could not make my hands blind,* he wrote. *This delicate body his hands caressed was indeed that of a woman, although she was not for me. I washed her, but I did not caress her. For me she was untouchable. My hands stopped short on her sides at the first faint swelling of her breasts. My body trembled, but it was with cold. She made no advances to me; she never said one word that could not have been equally well said in your presence. She has never tried to get anything from me. She has never been consciously aware of the problem—and until very recently neither had I! For me she was—still is, indeed, even now I know the truth and am torn with pity for her—something sacred and desexualized. These last few summers have been one long torment for me. I had tasted sensual pleasures when I was far away from you, in Europe. I longed for them day and night; but these wretched village girls are so scared of being strangled, with their own pigtails, by some father or brother whose primitive code of honor has to be defended that I never even thought of trying anything with them. I could not sleep. I would lie there naked on my rumpled bedclothes, body straining in a void, and*

*think of all the girls I would soon be seeing again.
Sometimes I used to get into the same state during
the day, and when this happened I would take a
solitary walk up to the nuraghe. She often used to
ask me, suspiciously, what on earth I was after
there. You ought to remember—once or twice, in
her innocence, she questioned me when you were
present. In fact I wanted to be alone there to have
fantasies about the girls I knew, girls I wanted and
would shortly be going back to. My violent physical desire gave me such strength and energy I
would run all the way up there. When I reached
the top I would fling off my clothes—oh, yes, I am
her son all right, I admit that—and lie there looking out over the sea.*

The Sardegra nuraghe still rises, after three
millennia, to a height of nearly fifty feet, and its
walls are some twenty-eight feet thick at the base.
Tall grasses sprout on its summit, and tall-
stemmed plants with clustering flowers—like
chandeliers with every bulb alight—wave there
in the breeze against a backdrop of blue sky.
Sweet-smelling herbs, all loud with bees, thrust
up from between the vast fine-grained blocks. Inside it is warm and dry and shaded, except for a
few shafts of sunlight lancing through cracks in
the stonework. The spiral staircase is built into the
wall itself, Cyclopean blocks piled up toward a
false vault constructed from still larger slabs. The
sand beneath the central dome shows traces of
footprints. Niches have been cut at intervals in the
wall, on the left-hand side of anyone trying to
negotiate the galleries—a neat and treacherous
device. From this vantage point a single defender,

with his boar's-tusk helmet and bronze sword, could run any assailant through his exposed side and block the entrance to the passage with the bodies of the first three enemies he struck down. At a certain point the vault suddenly becomes much lower, making it impossible to proceed any further except on all fours. A hollow, empty, wind-scoured place, where the air is always heavy with the scent of aromatic herbs.

Even when he was a child, Michael often used to go up and play there, all by himself. Doubtless this was for freedom, to get away from the loving yet overwhelming presence of his family. It was the one place he could do as he pleased. I can visualize him there all too easily, but with sadness. I see the great swag-bellied tower, a truncated cone made from blocks each as tall as a man, warm in the sunlight, and Michael standing with his back against it, his face a blank, lips compressed, eyes staring and perhaps showing signs of distress, while that big blond body of his—svelte, muscular, golden-haired—rises tall and ithyphallic above the lonely sea.

YOU HAVE never been able to see yourself from the outside, Marie, Carl-Gustav wrote. You had no idea what you looked like when you suddenly began to get so worked up and argued until you were out of breath. She was telling Carl-Gustav he had to remove Michael from boarding school and keep him at home. The boy could not help getting into bad company. Something awful was going to happen to him. She had a presentiment about it, she insisted. She couldn't sleep for worry. If Carl-Gustav loved her—above all, if he loved Michael—it was vital to save him. At the very least it was imperative that he be sent elsewhere, if possible to some country other than Switzerland. For there, she said, he was quite certainly getting into horrible company. Yes, that was the word: horrible. Her maternal instinct enabled her to sense the truth. After all, she was the boy's mother; she knew him better than anyone. She could not be more specific, she made no claim to know all the details. It was just an instinct on her part, but all the same this instinct was infallible: there must be no more shilly-shallying; it was absolutely essential to get him away from there—

Why didn't you tell me he had fallen in love? Carl-Gustav wrote. Why didn't you speak openly to me? Surely this was the one time you should have been absolutely frank and told me everything? But this would have meant your admitting something you neither could nor would admit. It would have meant stripping your soul bare, humiliating yourself before me. The truth of the matter is that, for the first time, your body—that divine garment with which you identified yourself—concealed something more than emptiness. You chose instead to go on living in my company, but isolated now just as I was. You could have saved him. You could have saved all three of us—at least, what was left for the saving. As it was, you merely reinforced my suspicions. Oh, yes, I thought you were both guilty, which in fact you weren't—at least, he wasn't. Your case, my love, is something else again.

116

IT HAD happened quite recently, during Michael's last vacation. *To whom should I tell the truth,* he wrote, *if not to her? You had been hostile for so long already I would never have dared confide in you.* He had to talk to Freya. And it was then that Michael found himself confronted with what he had long known but could never bring himself to admit openly. He had waited till summer was nearly over and the date of his departure at hand. *Now I understand why. It was because I knew, without daring to formulate the idea consciously, that the knowledge would hurt her, she could not accept it. But I was too happy in the knowledge of loving and being loved to understand or be capable of understanding anything except my own personal exaltation.*

And in the very act of unburdening himself to Freya, he saw her for the first time. He realized she was getting older. *It was as though she had aged a whole generation there in front of my eyes.*

She was sitting in a basket chair that stood against the wall of the house. He was shattered by her slovenly posture—hunched up, shoulders drooping, knees vulgarly spread under a too-short dress, feet turned in toward each other. *Freya,* of all people! She seemed lost in concentration. He felt his words falling flatly to the ground like so many tiny uninflated balloons. She was gnawing the nail of one index finger.

She said, "But you can't possibly love this—this *woman.*"

"She isn't a woman, darling. She's a young girl."

Freya repeated, with some asperity, "You can't love her and me at the same time."

He began to say something, but she interrupted him.

"You can't love two people at once! You don't love me."

"Of course I do, darling," Michael said. "I love you just as I've always loved you, just as I always will. It isn't the same thing—"

She appeared not to have heard what he said, let alone have understood. With dull obstinacy she said again, "You can't love her and me at the same time." Then she began to bite the nail of her middle finger. Freya biting her nails was unthinkable. Michael was astonished.

"But, darling," he insisted, in some puzzlement, "I keep telling you, *it isn't the same thing!* For heaven's sake."

And with the smile of an attentive courtier, he gallantly quoted a verse of D'Annunzio's. It was typical of Freya to have a weakness for D'Annunzio. He knew she adored being wooed in this way —indeed, had come to expect it of him, since she herself had trained him to the habit.

"*Fedra indimenticàbile,*" he murmured. "You are just as unforgettable—but, thank God, darling, you are *not* Phaedra, you are my beloved Freya. Anyway, she was only Hippolytus' stepmother, and you're my real mother—"

"Spare me your idiotic excuses, please," she said, cuttingly. "This isn't a literary discussion."

He stopped, thunderstruck. "You hate me," said Freya, hissing. "You've never really loved me—"

Her expression was so stubborn, so willfully obtuse, that I scarcely recognized her. I felt scared, I can tell you! Michael wrote. Freya was speaking in a kind of monologue, which she delivered star-

ing straight ahead into empty space. "You are being unfaithful to me. You already have been unfaithful to me. *You have discussed me with her,*"
in a tone of absolute assurance, just as though she
had been present during the discussion and participated in a scene that clearly filled her with unbearable revulsion.

"Well, of course—I told her how much I admire
and love you, what a unique person you are, how
proud I am to be your son!"

*None of this meant a thing to her. All she was
concerned with was the confirmation of her suspicion. Her face had gone a dirty gray color, which
scared me more than ever.*

With grim insistence she repeated, "You've
always hated me! You want to go away! You want
to tear yourself away by force—"

"No, it's not true—I'd never—"

But she was no longer listening. She got up and
left. He followed her "a little later" and looked for
her, first, in the house though he knew he would
not find her there, had no wish to find her, was
thoroughly scared, and wanted to run away—
something he only realized later. Then, after
Assunta had assured him that the *signora* had
gone that way, he set off on the track up to the
nuraghe. *I did not find her,* he wrote. But when he
reached the foot of the nuraghe itself, he heard
the sound of weeping inside. Her loud hysterical
sobs echoed and reechoed through the central
vault in that great mass of masonry, blending into
one long ululation that ran around the galleries,
up and down the spiral stairs. But the sheer thick-
ness of the walls deadened the noise; from outside
you could hear it only if you were very close.

I was afraid. I had been afraid ever since the beginning of our knowing it. I have been continually afraid ever since. For her; of her. I was a coward. Instead of going into the tower and comforting her—yet how could one have gone about it? and would she have let herself be comforted, by me of all people?—I went away, as I did on that other occasion, when I saw what I should never have seen. I left her alone and walked back down to the house.

From that day on, she did not speak to him. She no longer spoke at the table. She took long solitary walks. *I know where she goes,* Michael wrote. *She climbs up to the nuraghe, goes inside it, and cries her eyes out, all by herself. You do understand, Father, don't you? I've got to go. I have no alternative. Please forgive me. I didn't mean this to happen. Nor did she. She still knows nothing. She's a sick woman. We ought to feel sorry for her. We've got to be patient and wait for her to forget all this nonsense. I don't intend to show my face here again. Later, perhaps. Much later. Now I—*

AT THIS POINT Michael was interrupted by Ignazia calling him. She came in looking very mysterious, as only a simple country peasant can, and proceeded to drag him not only out of his room but out of the house just, in her own words, "to give him a message from the *signora.*" The heap of manuscript was left lying there on the table; Michael thought he would be away only a moment or so.

WHY DID you never tell me he wanted to make a break from us—from you, rather? Carl-Gustav wrote. *I would have acted differently then. I would only have felt resentment against you, not him. But the truth is that he meant very little more to you than I did. The only person you are really concerned with is yourself—your own power, your ability to dominate. You could not let him off the hook. But this time you went too far. You'd been overdoing it for a long while. Too long. I couldn't stand it any more. You'll understand me, I'm sure. In the end I weakened. I yielded to my crazy, delectable temptation and had a little talk with Lupu. Whether he's sick or a victim of social circumstances, I neither know nor care. He is always ready for anything; all he needs is some slight ideological justification and a reasonable chance of getting away with it.*

He had incited Lupu to do the deed during one of their nocturnal discussions, when it was dark enough for neither of them to see the other's face.

"Tell me, Lupu—" he began. Lupu stood with his back against the wall, by the open doorway, feet crossed, his hands thrust deep in his pockets, waiting.

"What do you do here if—well, if a man sees that something is going on between his wife and his son?"

Silence.

"Between mother and son. Such things do happen sometimes, don't they?"

"Sometimes," Lupu said. "But not often. Almost never."

"Almost never, perhaps. But if it *does* happen?"

Lupu remained silent for a long time. Then he

said, "You know very well what the man must do."

Another silence fell. These were not real questions; Lupu's replies were not real answers.

"And justice?"

Lupu shrugged in the darkness. "That *is* justice."

"No, I mean people, public opinion—"

Lupu sneered. "People are astonished that *one* has done nothing for so long."

"But what about the police—the courts—?"

"Oh, them." Lupu's voice was scornful and dismissive. "This is nothing to do with them. It concerns no one else."

They both fell silent for a little. Neither of them moved. The air in the room never stirred. Not a sound from the terrace.

"In our country," Carl-Gustav said finally, "such a thing could never happen. No one would do it. No one."

Lupu gave a brief snort of laughter. "You mean you let them get away with it where you come from?" He hawked and spat—not onto the terrace, but there on the floor of the room, something he had never done before.

Carl-Gustav was finding it harder and harder to talk, to articulate each successive word, despite the shadows that hid his face.

"Where I come from—my kind of person— never—" His voice trailed away.

"*Gente ricca,*" Lupu said. "*Gente dabbene.* We're different. Peasants. Have to do everything for ourselves."

Silence fell once more. I shall not say another word, Carl-Gustav decided. Then Lupu coughed and said roughly, "Him or her?"

Carl-Gustav felt the sweat begin to trickle out

122

of every pore, roll down his cheeks in heavy drops. In a still, small voice he said, "What do *you* suggest? What would happen here?"

Lupu thought for a moment, his face still invisible. At length he said, "Him first." Then he added, "To make her weep for him."

Carl-Gustav said nothing. He could feel the sweat chilling on his back and under his armpits. Lupu said, "Well, is that what you want?"

Carl-Gustav shrank back in his leather armchair, and the wooden frame creaked. I won't say it, he thought. There's no need. He'll understand. At least I won't have spoken the word.

Lupu neither spoke nor moved; he simply stood there waiting. At last, when the silence and tension had become quite unbearable, Carl-Gustav said in a strangulated voice, "Yes."

Another silence. Lupu began to cough again. Then he said in a matter-of-fact way, "I used to make toys for him when he was a kid."

It was a plain statement of fact. Carl-Gustav had not made toys for Michael; Lupu had. He said no more. There was not even the sound of breathing. This was the longest silence of all. Now it was up to Lupu to make his decision. At last he gave a kind of grunt and disappeared without saying a word. Only the open door bore witness to his presence.

THE LAST summer storm had been gathering for some time. All the warning signs were there: dry and stifling heat, tension in the air, brief red flashes over the darkened sea, followed by muted rolls of thunder from somewhere high behind the hills.

Freya, who had not spoken to anyone for days, now became the life and soul of the dinner table, laughing and chattering gaily. Michael played up to her mood, but with obvious surprise and embarrassment. Carl-Gustav was bored and looked it. After dinner he sat down with a tome on the neolithic village of Skara Brae and began to leaf through the illustrations by the light of a sputtering pressure lamp. *The way it sputtered,* he wrote, *made me want to pick it up, lift it above my head with both hands, and smash it to pieces on the floor. If it caught fire and burned the house down, so much the better. But I am a phlegmatic person, not given to demonstrations of that sort, and neither of you noticed a thing. She was too busy flashing you radiant private glances, smiling at you in a way that revealed those brilliant white teeth of hers; and you—poor Michael!—looked the soul of shamefaced embarrassment. This strange flirtatious mood was something quite new—intense, nervous, tentative—and you had no idea how to cope with it.*

"I need a breath of fresh air," Freya said brightly. "Like to come for a walk with me, up to the nuraghe? Oh, come on! If you don't, I'll just have to go by myself."

Michael glanced at his father. Carl-Gustav smiled amiably. Later, in order to punish and torture himself, he recorded this fact when writing to Freya. *I smiled amiably at him,* he wrote. Aloud he said, "Of course—off you go, you can't let her traipse up there all on her own."

"Let's go then," Freya exclaimed. She seized

Michael's hand and rushed out into the hot, still night, where the foliage hung like stone, brooding, expectant. They reached the top amazingly quickly, considering how dark it was. They ran all the way and were out of breath when they got there. *Her hand clutched mine so tightly,* Michael wrote, *that for a moment I was astonished to find she had such sheer strength in her fingers.* This was in the middle of his letter, where he begged his father to believe that nothing happened between them that he, Carl-Gustav, could not have witnessed with perfect propriety.

Just as they reached the top of the rise, a bolt of lightning lit up the nuraghe. For an instant they glimpsed its huge, squat bulk, glowing a dull red against the night, ringed with bushes, wearing its floral crown of herbs and tall blossoming tapers. Everything was absolutely still; not a leaf or twig or petal stirred anywhere. Then there was nothing but the night again, deep and impenetrable. Two or three big warm drops fell on their heads and upturned faces. A moment later the rain was pouring down in torrents. It got very cold. In seconds they were soaked through to the bone. A tremendous gust of wind nearly blew them off their feet. It was followed by a second, and a third, each more violent than its predecessor.

The branches of the trees thrashed and tossed and leaves came down in showers. Some of them brushed Michael's face. He stood there staring at Freya. They were still holding hands. Her eyes never left his. They were huge, dilated, gleaming bright in the darkness. Her fingers continued to clasp his far too tightly.

He wanted to tell her they could take shelter in

the nuraghe. She may have guessed this from his expression, the way he glanced for an instant toward the low entrance, a still blacker patch against the night. Freya followed his gaze and shouted something. *I couldn't make out what she was saying.* Michael wrote. *The noise was deafening, and anyway I rather think she was having difficulty getting the words out. In fact. I'm pretty sure she wasn't making coherent sense at all.*

Suddenly a convulsion shook her. He felt it pass through their clasped hands and spread through his own body. Freya cried out again, a piercing scream this time, and wrenched her hand violently away from Michael's. There was something so quick and abrupt about the way she turned and fled that she might almost have been a wild animal. She was running now, away from Michael, away from the nuraghe. Michael, without knowing why, set off in pursuit of her. They went stumbling and skidding down the path. *I was scared she might fall and do herself some injury,* Michael wrote, *but I couldn't catch up with her.* Perhaps he was really scared; perhaps he preferred not to catch up with her. She was certainly going too fast for someone who wanted to be caught.

She was going too fast, in great flying leaps, and uttering shrill little screams all the time. The noise resembled wild, hysterical laughter. Michael found himself laughing too, for no reason, *as a result of the nervous excitement brought on by the storm.*

Far below them, the house appeared and vanished in a succession of lightning flashes. Between peals of thunder the sea could be heard; it was visible too, for brief moments, gray and storm-tossed, seething angrily in the darkness. Rain hissed down through the sodden undergrowth, trickling into every crack in the ground, pouring down the hollow worn paths, so that the ravine was soon full to the brim and in roaring spate.

They were out of breath when they got back. Water ran off Freya in streams; her dress clung to her naked body. Her eyes were almost too bright; her face was very pale, except for a fleck of high color on each cheekbone. She was still laughing and had Michael in tow behind her. He too was naked under his rain-drenched clothes. He looked pale and haggard *and would not meet my eye. You had taken a long time,* Carl-Gustav wrote. *Weren't you surprised to find Lupu with me, to find both of us standing there waiting for you? Yet why should you have been surprised? For you I was nonexistent, and Lupu less than nothing. Nor was I surprised when he turned up at the house, the shoulders of his coat sodden-black with rain, and said, in that flat voice of his, "You have to find shelter somewhere when you're caught out of doors in weather like this." "In the nuraghe," I said. "Yes," he said, with a nasty little smile, "there's nice fine sand on the floor there."*

It was only after you had both gone off to change your clothes that he looked directly at me. I nodded my head affirmatively. He went out without another word and—in conformity with his new practice—without bidding me goodnight. Why did you not tell me, Marie? Why wouldn't you consciously acknowledge what had happened to you, what it was you wanted, what you were doing?

I CAN picture the exchange between Michael and Ignazia in the middle of the courtyard. He stood there, very tall and straight, half-naked—he was wearing nothing but shorts, not even a pair of sandals—with his statue-smooth torso and fine, heavily muscled legs, dark gold hair glinting on his forearms where the sun struck it, head forward. His nose was too short, and he had his father's lopsided mouth, that slight twist to the upper lip that always gave him a slightly sulky air. His eyes, high-set beneath that strong forehead, were still and expressionless, almost like those of a blind man.

He was bending down from his great height toward Ignazia. The hunchback's puny body was, as always, wrapped in a variety of garments, black or brown or dark blue. The one remarkable feature in her flat, swarthy, peasant face was her eyes, which sparkled with vivacity. Yet she had this quality completely under control; she could turn it on or off at will. She looked up at him now, smiling her bright malicious smile, scrutinizing his face with avid curiosity. But Michael remained his usual taciturn, phlegmatic, expressionless self.

"*Signorino,*" she said, "the *signora* says you are to go and wait for her up on the Giara."

"He hesitated," Ignazia said later. "He disliked the idea. He didn't want to go." (Despite all evidence to the contrary, she never retracted her story, but swore "it was true the *signora* had told her.") He hesitated. He disliked the idea. Perhaps he was distressed at the thought of this meeting. But he could not bring himself to disobey Freya. He was still—for what little time remained to him —her little slave boy. The bus did not pass through

128

till late in the afternoon. He could have taken his father's old Ford, without asking permission. But from what I knew of him, I feel sure he would have found this small breach of good manners wholly repugnant. He was too proud, too clumsy, and far too slow in his reactions to take anything on the spur of the moment, without careful thought. (Ignazia used to say of him, "The *signorino* was a good boy, *ma un po' stùpido*.") Any other teen-ager in his position would have taken off at once—indeed, long before—and on foot, if need be. But Michael was still something of a child and far too closely attached to his home and family.

He glanced over Ignazia's shoulder and saw Freya's tall blond silhouette, moving along behind the low hedge that divided the court into two halves, the one with the pond and the chopping block, the other reserved for the Enquists' private use.

"Why can't she tell me herself?" Michael asked coldly.

Ignazia laughed soundlessly, barely showing her flat teeth. Small lines of amusement crinkled her worn cheeks.

"I don't know," she said. "Maybe she doesn't want the *professore* to know."

Michael reddened. Then he turned, crossed the courtyard, and took the path that led to the nuraghe and the plateau beyond. Ignazia could still see him for a while, threading his way through the vines and the *maquis;* as he dwindled into the distance, he must have seemed to emanate from them, to be their emanation made flesh, and exquisitely luminous flesh in the bargain. It was a beautiful day of mild sunshine; the sky was blue and still dewy-fresh, like a spring morning.

Freya had also noticed him and now came through to the yard. She tried to call him, but he was already out of earshot.

"Where's he off to?" she asked Ignazia.

Ignazia began to laugh. Her laugh was two-dimensional; it pulled her mouth into an oblong that had no depth. She said, "He told me he was going for a stroll up on the Giara."

Freya frowned in nervous irritation. "But he won't be back in time for lunch—"

"If the *signora* wishes," Ignazia said, watching her narrowly, "I could run after him and—"

"Yes, do that, will you? Tell him I expect him back in time for lunch." When Ignazia was already some way up the track, Freya called after her, "You'll find him somewhere around the nuraghe!"

Without turning around Ignazia picked up her skirts and set off up the fork toward the tower. "I'll be expecting him!" Freya shouted. Later she repeated the same phrase—not "*We'll* be expecting him," but "*I'll* be expecting him."

Ignazia walked slower and slower. She had no intention of overtaking Michael. She followed him at a good distance, often losing sight of him, until he emerged on the plateau itself. Then she spotted him again, a tall, broad-shouldered silhouette against the pale blue of the sky, very slim and erect, head haloed with gold.

Then, abruptly, he stopped. Another silhouette, dark and squat, had appeared in front of him, out of the bushes. The curve of the hill meant that only the tops of these bushes were visible from where he stood. Ignazia crouched down behind a clump of thornbushes and watched them intently.

CARL-GUSTAV and Freya had lunch alone, without speaking to one another. Neither of them had any appetite. At last Freya threw down her table napkin and said, "Where *is* he, for heaven's sake? What in the world can he be up to? *You* don't know, I suppose?"

Carl-Gustav looked at her gravely. Heavy drinking over a period of years had turned the whites of his eyes yellow and the pupils a blurred bluish-gray. He shook his head and said, with very precise enunciation, "Not exactly."

Freya sprang to her feet and began to pace around the room.

"*Not exactly!* The expressions you use! Can't you talk like an ordinary person and say *I don't know?* Where *is* he, for God's sake, *where is he?* What on earth is he playing at?"

I kept my eyes lowered, Carl-Gustav wrote. *I was reserving the pleasure of scrutinizing your reactions for slightly later. I was wrong. This was the last occasion I would ever see you, and I did not realize it. I'm sorry about that. I'm sorry. I'm sorry.*

Freya could not relax. She went out and interrogated Assunta and Giusta. Neither of them could tell her a thing. The men were working in the fields. They themselves had seen nothing, heard nothing. Freya returned to the house and went into Michael's room. She found his unfinished letter, sat down, and read it.

131

For a long time the house was absolutely quiet. Carl-Gustav had gone back to his work room and sat there, motionless. At last he heard Freya call, or rather scream, his name. *It was a very disagreeable sound,* he noted. *Raucous. Masculine.* She burst into the room and threw down the blue sheets of Michael's letter. Her lips opened, but for a moment the words would not come; she stood there, mouthing them, one finger pointing at the scattered pages.

At last she burst out, "He's gone, and it's all your fault! Look what you've done! Bring him back to me, do you hear? *Bring him back to me!*"

Ashen-faced, trembling with misery and rage, she shook her fist in Carl-Gustav's face and screamed, "Don't just sit there like a cretin! Can't you understand? He's gone! Because of *you,* and your filthy jealousy! Get up, go and find him, this instant! Bring him back to me!" Her voice cracked with hysterical fury; she seized Carl-Gustav by the shoulders and shook him, but his huge frame was heavy, resistant, inert.

"Come now, control yourself," he said. Instinctively he had begun to sort and stack the sheets.

She rushed to the door. He could hear her still screaming outside in the courtyard, but by now he had begun to read. This letter came as a complete surprise to him.

Ignazia appeared, panting with emotion and exhaustion. She seemed drained, and at the same time grimly excited. She had clearly been running. By now it was afternoon, and all the fresh greens and blues of the morning had been dried out by sun and wind.

"*Signora! Signora!*" she shouted.

Freya hurried toward her.

132

"*Signora,* something's happened. The young master—he's had an accident. He's in a very bad way—"

Freya grabbed her arm and shook it violently. "What's happened to him?" she screamed. "Where is he?"

"Up there—he's lying on the ground. I couldn't lift him. He's far too big and heavy—"

"Carl-Gustav!" Freya shouted. "Where are you? Something's happened to the child!"

Now she was appealing to him. Something had happened to the child. But it was quite a time before he appeared, and when he did "it was obvious," as Ignazia put it afterward, "that the *professore* had already had more than enough to drink." Freya did not wait for him. She never saw him again. She was running, dragging a slow and protesting Ignazia behind her.

"*Signora,* I'm dead tired. I've been walking for hours—please, I can't go so fast! You go on in front," she gasped. "I'll catch up with you."

Freya threw off Ignazia's small, brown, bony fist as if it were some object to be tossed away, disposed of, and began to run at a tremendous speed. Ignazia followed her, but more and more slowly, until at last she stopped and rested for a moment—after which she picked up her skirts and went bounding back down the track to the village, leaping from step to step like a mountain goat.

I HAVE a friend who is a native of Oristano. One day, I remember, when we were discussing these high, lonely, undulating plateaus—I cannot remember which one provoked the remark, it may have been either the Giara di Serri or the Giara di Gesturi—he burst out, "But there's nothing there! *Non c'è niente, assolutamente niente!"*

In one sense he was right, and the remark was equally true of the Giara de Lunas. There *was* nothing up there, save barren windswept uplands. The only signs of life were occasional shepherds' huts, conelike erections of unmortised stone, with smoke from the hearth fires seeping through cracks in the roof capping; and beside them the sheep pens, and middens, great piles of dry black sheep droppings the size of olives, with that rank smell so like the odor of unwashed wool, still impregnated with the sweat of the beast it came from. Nothing else but solitude and silence, an occasional buzzard circling high overhead, and here and there, scattered in the grass, tiny white picked bones or a hare's skull, still with a pair of furry ears the fox would not touch. Nothing and nobody, as far as the eye can reach.

In spring the grass is tender and succulent, a lush green carpet. Cyclamens open to reveal their radiant inner fire, sweet-smelling rock roses glow bright in the sunshine, and tall asphodels—the plant known to antiquity as *herba sardonica*—wave in the wind. The asphodel was credited with various poisonous properties, among them the cause of a special kind of madness that, it was said, was characterized by wild, frenetic gaiety and uncontrollable outbursts of joyless laughter. The ants scurrying among the lichen-grown blocks of lava must be permanently drunk with the blended aroma of mint, benjamin, and thyme. If you lie down here you will soon fall asleep, lulled and drugged by their subtle, pungent odor.

But that day was near the beginning of autumn; everything was dry and withered, plants drooped lifelessly, and the very soil, long calcined by the sun, blew hither and thither in clouds of dust, leaving the earth bald and sterile. Already the wind had a chill in it; hill paths were stripped down to their bare, hard-baked clay subsoil. It was on such a track that Michael stopped when he saw Lupu rise up in front of him. I have been there and seen the spot where it happened. There really was nothing there, nothing at all. The rains, which used this path about as often—or as seldom—as the shepherds, had turned it into a shallow drain, with a bed of grayish-yellow clay. Farther on was the clump of thornbushes where Lupu had lain in ambush, well out of sight, waiting for the appearance of that tall fair figure and then springing up ten paces in front of it. Beyond, the barren landscape receded in a series of shallow undulating ridges. The horizon was quite close, a low, flattened line. But there was always a slightly higher point somewhere—a clump of rough bushes, a few blackish standing boulders—that would serve as cover and from which someone, lying flat on stomach and elbows, quite still and with no particular object in mind, was sure to be observing you.

So the hidden watchers must have seen those two silhouettes stand face to face for a moment. They were shepherds and were trained to hold their tongues. They saw the quick movement of two arms bringing up a gun to the firing position, saw the long black barrel blossom with a cloud of smoke that the constant wind scouring the plateau blew instantly away, just as it muffled the sound of the shot. Everything happened silently, and yet it was not silence, but the wind.

CARL-GUSTAV was reading the letter over again when a shadow momentarily blocked the doorway. He looked up and saw Lupu, lounging in his favorite position against the doorpost, and eying him with the usual stony-faced effrontery.

I felt myself blushing, Carl-Gustav wrote. *I have not blushed for thirty years or more. Now, I suppose, I had something to blush about.*

He cleared his throat. "What did he say?" he asked, in a high, unnatural voice.

"Nothing." Lupu paused. "There was nothing to say."

With a curiously detached astonishment, Carl-Gustav became aware that tears were trickling down his cheeks. Later he noted down the fact in his letter to Freya, again with the same expression of surprise. *This was the first occasion on which I experienced this particular type of distress. It was extremely unpleasant. Since then it has recurred.*

"Was he afraid?" he asked.

"Oh, yes," Lupu said. "He was afraid. Who wouldn't have been afraid?"

"But he said nothing?"

"No, nothing. He just stood there. Like an ox." Lupu was watching his employer with cruel intentness. *He must have thought exactly the same of me,* Carl-Gustav wrote.

Slowly Carl-Gustav's expression changed. So did Lupu's. He seemed unable to tear his eyes away from his master's face. But gradually the intentness ebbed, leaving a blank behind. Lupu's features wavered uncertainly. Then he quickly turned his face toward the door, lowered his head, hunching it between his shoulders, gave an abrupt groan, or grunt, like a frightened animal starting out of the way, and rushed off.

Later, almost without noticing it, Carl-Gustav threw up. He had been in the same position for some while, lying there with his cheek and temple resting on the table, whimpering quietly to himself. Now he got up and, not even bothering to wipe his mouth, went in search of something to drink. He went on swallowing alcohol until he felt he was on the point of passing out. Then he left the house, and staggered off up the path his wife and son had taken.

THE VILLAGE women had been alerted by Ignazia and turned out en masse, a straggling black and brown swarm. It was they who found Freya up on the plateau, about the middle of that cold, windy afternoon. Her bare-armed body, still in that light summer dress, was lying on Michael's, her blond hair falling loose over his face. From time to time, without emitting a sound, she would run her fingers blindly over him, press herself closer against his frame, now oddly flattened by the loss of all nervous tonicity. She crouched astride him, pressed him under her, sought for him still. She was alone on this beaten earth track, surrounded by a ring of silent watching women.

At last one of them—no one admitted to knowing which, and perhaps she herself was never

137

aware of it—picked up a stone, rose to her full height, and threw it with all her strength.

The Giara is littered with stones: rough, shapeless, lichen-stained lumps, just the right size to fit one's hand.

Freya did not recoil or shudder when the stone struck her. She did not appear to notice. After the third or fourth she raised her head; but even then she barely seemed aware that she was not alone. "She didn't understand," they said afterward. She let her head fall back, and her hair covered Michael's face. After a little she must surely have felt pain. But she did not suffer long. The stones hailed down thick and fast, and the peasant women kept stooping to pick up more. As they struck they made an audible sound, sometimes sharp, sometimes a dull thud.

When Carl-Gustav reached the spot, no one was there but Michael and Freya. Some shepherds, watching from a distance, reported later that the Swedish *signore* had stood there for some time, his eyes fixed on the two corpses at his feet. Then he too went away.